KUSAMAKURA

NATSUME SŌSEKI

translated by
TAKAHASHI KAZUTOMO

Publisher : BoD · Books on Demand, 31 avenue Saint-Rémy, 57600 Forbach, bod@bod.fr
Print : Libri Plureos GmbH, Friedensallee 273, 22763 Hamburg (Allemagne)
ISBN : 978-2-3225-7013-3
Dépôt légal : Juin 2025

PREFACE

Kinnosuke Natsume, better known by his pen-name "Sōseki," was one of, if not, greatest fiction writers, modern Japan has produced. A man of solid university education unlike many another of the fraternity, he established a school of his own, in point of originality in style, and what is more important, in the angle from which he observed human affairs. More points of difference about him from others were the complete absence in his case of romantic elements and adversities, almost always inseparable from the early life of literary geniuses, and the sudden blazing into fame from obscurity, except as a popular school teacher and then a university professor, with some partiality for the hokku school of poetry.

Sōseki Natsume was born in January, 1867, a third son of an old family in Kikui-cho, Tokyo. His education after a primary school course took a deviation, for some years, into the old-fashioned study of Chinese classics. It was probably then that he laid foundation, perhaps unknown to himself, of the development of his literary talent, that later blossomed out so picturesquely; and he was different, also, in this respect from the later Meiji era writers, who went, many of them, through a Christian mission school, and were all under the influence of Western literature.

In 1884, our future novelist entered the Yobimon College, intending to become an architect; but later changing his mind he took a course in the Literature Department of Tokyo Imperial University, from which he graduated in 1892. While in the university, Sōseki formed a close friendship with Shiki Masaoka, which lasted until the latter's death separated them in 1904. Shiki Masaoka was the greatest figure in the revival of hokku poetry in rejuvenated Japan, and Sōseki's association with him accounts for the novelist's mastery of that branch of literature.

After finishing his postgraduate course in the university in 1895, Kinnosuke Natsume taught successively in Matsuyama Middle School in Iyo, and the Fifth High School in Kumamoto, making no name particularly for himself except as a bright, promising scholar. He took a wife unto himself in 1896, and was four years later sent by the Government to England to study English literature. In three years he returned home to be appointed Lecturer in Tokyo Imperial University. About this time his "London Letters" in Shiki Masaoka's Hokku magazine, the *Hototogisu*, began to attract attention; but it was not till the publication of the first book of maiden work *I Am a Cat*, that he suddenly entered the temple of fame. That was in 1905.

The *Cat* with its perfect novelty of conception, style, study of human nature, etc., made him, at once, a star of first magnitude in the literary firmament, and from that time on, for the next five years, his productions, long and short, followed in a constant stream, including *Botchan* (Innocent in Life); *Kusamakura* (Unhuman Tour); *Sanshiro*; *Kofu* (The Miner); *Hinageshi* (The Corn-Poppy) and many others, some, perhaps many, of which are assured an immortal life.

Soon after his debut as a fiction writer with meteoric brilliance, Sōseki resigned his post at Tokyo Imperial University and also First High School, and accepted a position in the Tokyo *Asahi Shimbun* (newspaper) Office as its literary editor. Five years later he was seized with ulceration of the stomach, from which he never really recovered, and he died in December, 1916.

If Sōseki's rise to fame was meteoric, his retention of it was also meteoric, it lasting only five years, before he bowed to an illness that sent him to the grave in another five years.

All of Sōseki's writings have a ring distinctly his own and are pervaded by a vein of thought, which is the happiest combination of humour born of poetical acumen and well meaning cynicism of the human heart. Especially is this true of *Kusamakura* or "The Pillow of Grass," which is a poetical way in Japanese of speaking of a journey or tour, and is rendered into "Unhuman Tour" in the present translation, from its contents rather than its literal meaning.

In *Kusamakura*, Sōseki is at his best in giving free play to his artistic fancies and contempt for conventional worldliness, to visualise a refined Bohemianism, if there be such a thing, by summoning all his literary skill. How his dissertations on his own dreamy fancies, occurring frequently in the story, will take with the Western readers is problematical; but they most fascinatingly appeal to the Japanese mind, which always takes the highest delight in things that are presented with philoso-poetical humour. *Kusamakura* was the most successful of Sōseki's work, second only to *I Am a Cat.*

It should be added that the present translator is not conceited enough to think that his English version, which nearly covers the whole original text of *Kusamakura*, is doing anything like justice to the master strokes of its creator. He considers himself well repaid for his labor, if he succeeds in giving an idea of the trend of thought and atmosphere which Sōseki loved to produce and for which he is so ardently liked by his countrymen.

It is to be added that no attempt has been made at versification in translating poems of all kind, but to barely transliterate the original.

TRANSLATOR.

Tokyo, June 21, 1927.

KUSAMAKURA
UNHUMAN TOUR

I

Climbing the mountain, I was caught up into a train of thought.

Work with your brains, and you are liable to be harsh. Punt in the stream of sentiment, and you may be carried away. Pride stiffens you to discomfort. Heigh-ho, this is a disagreeable world to live in. When the disagreeableness deepens, you wish to move to a world where life is less uneasy. It is precisely when you awake to the truth, that move where you will, it will be hard to live, that poetry is born and art creates.

This human world of ours is the making neither of God nor of the Devil; but of common mortals; your neighbors on your right; your neighbors on your left, and your neighbors across the street. Hate you may this world of common mortals, but where else can you go? If anywhere else, it must be an unhuman world, but you will find an unhuman world a worse place to live in than this of humanity. Things being disagreeable in the world you cannot depart from it, but you must resign yourself to making the best of disagreeableness, by rubbing off its sharp corners and relaxing its pinches, to what degree you may, to pass pleasantly, even for a brief while, this life of so short a span. Here arises the heaven-ordained mission of the poet and the painter, and blessed are they, who with their art, make life in this world more rich and more cheerful.

Picture your hard-to-live-in-world, turned into one of bliss and thankfulness, with all its disagreeableness taken away, and you have poetry, a painting, or music, or sculpture. Nor need you produce it actually; when you fancy you see it before your eyes, poetry springs into life and songs arise. You hear the ringing of a silver bell within you, even though you have not written a line of your verse on paper, and your mind's eye drinks of the beauties of the rainbow without paint on the canvas. You attain your end as soon as you soar to the height of taking this view of the human life you live in and see the soiled and turbid latter-day world purified and beautified in your soul's camera obscura. Thus a poet may not have a single uttered verse and a painter not a solitary sweep of the brush; but they are happier than a social lion; than the most fondled child; nay, than a great prince, in that they can have their own cleansed view of life; in that they can rise above lust and passions, and live in a world of etherial purity; in that they can build up a universe where differences all disappear, and can break away free from the bondage of greed and selfishness.

Twenty years of life taught me that this is a world worth living in; at twenty-five I saw that light and darkness are but the face and back of a thing, there being a shadow where the sun shines. My thoughts, today, at thirty, are these: When full of joys sorrows are as deep, and the more pain the greater pleasure. Cut sorrows asunder from joys and I won't be able to get along. Shall I fling them away? that will make an end of the world. Money is precious; but anxiety will eat you up, even in sleep, when it accumulates. Love is sweet; but you will yearn after the days when you knew it not, so soon as its very sweetness begins to weigh heavy on you. The shoulders of His Majesty's Ministers are supporting the feet of millions and the whole country is weighing heavily on their backs. You miss nice things when you part with them without tasting; but you want more of them when you take only a little of them, while you get sick if you overload yourself....

Here my train of thought broke, as I found myself sitting involuntarily on a good-sized boulder, my left foot having, in its effort to avert a peril, caused by a slip of my right foot, landed me in that posture. Fortunately I was none the worse for the accident, except that my color-box jerked itself forward from under my arm, which was not much.

As I rose from my forced rest, I saw at a distance, to my right, a peak of mountain, the very shape of a bucket with its bottom up, covered from foot to summit by thick dark greens, studded with blossoming cherries in a dreamy relief, behind a screen of haze. A little nearer there rose a bare mountain, rising shoulders above the others, with its flank cut straight down as by a giant's axe. The foot of its craggy side sank into a dark abyss. A figure of man wrapped in a red blanket was coming down from the height and I thought my climb would have to take me up there. The road was very exasperating. If clay only, it would not have required such very great labor to negotiate, but there were boulders, which refused to be smoothed. Clay may be broken, but not rocks and there they lay determined not to give way. If unyielding on their part, then they must be passed by going round or else by surmounting them. The place was not easy to go up even without rocks; but to make it worse, it made a sharp angle in the centre, the sides of which rose sharply, so that it was more like walking the bed of a river than going up a road. However, not being in a particular hurry, I took time and slowly came up to the "Seven Bends."

As I trudged upward, my ears suddenly caught a lark, his song coming up, as it were, from just below my feet. The carol was giddily busy and incessant, but my eyes saw nothing. That bird never stops and must, it appears, sing out the whole Spring day and every second of it till night. I looked down the valley left and right into the air, and up into the sky, but all in vain, as the unseen singer was heard to rise higher and higher. I thought the lark must have died in the clouds and his song only was floating in space. The road made a sharp turn here by an angular rock. A blind man might have plunged head first down the crag. But I managed to turn safely. Down in the valley the golden blossoms of the rape were in full bloom.

But the lark! It was Spring—Spring, when the whole creation feels blasé to drowsiness; cheerful to ecstacy. The cat forgets to pounce on the mice. Men become oblivious of being in debt; so oblivious, indeed, that they even fail to locate their own souls. But they come back to themselves, when they see a distant field waving with a golden sea of flowers, such as I was looking down upon in the valley. And they may locate their souls when they hear the lark. The lark does not sing with his throat; but it is his whole soul that sings. Of all creatures, of which you hear their soul's activity in their songs, none is as lively as the lark. It was, indeed, joy itself, and as I thus thought, I became joyful, and thus, was Poetry.

Yes, poetry! Soon I was trying to repeat Shelley's song of the lark; but I could recite only these lines:

> "We look before and after
>   And pine for what is not:
> Our sincerest laughter
>   With pain is fraught;
> Our sweetest songs are those that tell of
>   saddest thought."

I once more lost myself in a reverie of thought. Happy as the poet may be, he may not go heart and soul into singing of his joys, forgetting everything, like the lark. The Chinese poets, to say nothing of their brothers of the West, sing of "immeasurable bushels of sorrow." It may be, with common mortals, that their sorrows are measured only by the pint not by the bushel. Who can say nay, then, if the poet soars to the height of joys unreachable by his vulgar brothers, he has also unfathomable griefs? It is perhaps, well, that one thinks twice before one decides to become a poet.

My eyes captivated by the golden rape on the left, a coppice hill on the right and the road under foot running on a smooth level, I stepped now and again on humble dandelions, crushing them, as I thought, under my heels; but on looking back regretfully, I found the lowly beauty nestling, none the worse, in their double-toothed leaves. Easy is the life of some of God's creations.

I continued my climb, returning again to my thoughts of reverie.

Sorrow may be inseparable from the poet. But once in an humour, in which you forget yourself, listening to a lark or gazing at a bed of golden rape, all gloom and pain disappear. Going along a mountain path so entranced, dandelions make your heart leap with joy. So do the blossoming cherries—the cherries had now gone out of sight, by the way. Up in the mountain, in the bosom of nature, everything that greets you fills your heart with joy, with not a shadow of misery. If any misery, it would be no more than that of feeling tired in your feet and of not having good things to eat.

But how can this be? Nature unrolls herself before you as a piece of poetry, as a scroll of a picture. Since poetry and a picture, no thought occurs to you of getting possession of this home of nature, nor a desire to make a scoup of money by making it accessible by building a railway. Nothing darkens this scenery, to rob it of its charms, which help neither to fill your belly, nor add something to your salary, as long as it gladdens your heart merely as scenery, so long shall you feel no pain, no weight on you. So great is the power of nature that it intoxicates you, transports you, in an instant, to the world of poetry.

Love may be beautiful, and so also filial devotion, and noble and edifying may be loyalty and patriotism. But it will be different when you are yourself a figure on the stage, a cyclone of conflicting interests making you too dizzy to appreciate the beautiful or the noble, but to become entirely lost to the poetry of the thing.

You have to make an onlooker of yourself with room for a sense to understand, in order that you may see the poetry. Placed in that position, you will enjoy dramas, and novels will interest you; because you have got your personal interests packed and put away on the rack. You are a poet the while you enjoy reading or seeing.

Even at that, common dramas and novels are not free from humanities of afflictions, anger, quarrels, and weeping, that carry you into corresponding moods. The only saving feature may be that no sense of gain and selfishness is acting on your part; but this absence of personal interest will make your heartstrings the more tense and active in other respects, and that is what I hate to bear.

I have come through my thirty years enough, indeed more than enough, of wallowing in the mud of troubles, of fuming in anger; of being in rows; or of sinking in sorrows; all which are indivorcible from human life. I want poetry that lifts me above the dust and noise of the world. I know, of course, there can be no drama, however great a masterpiece, that is absolutely transcendental of human sentiment, or scarcely a novel that can rise completely above all sense of right and wrong, this being especially the case with Western poetry of which the stock paraphernalia are Sympathy, Love, Justice, Freedom, and so forth, the staple goods in the bazaar of human life. It is no wonder that the lark made Shelly heave a deep sigh. To my joy, poets of the Orient can, some of them, soar above this earthly atmosphere. Let Tao Yuan-ming of ancient China recite his lines:

> "Chrysanthemum I pick from the Eastern
>   hedge,
>   On the Southern hill leisurely I cast my
>   eyes."

Not that there is a charming one on the other side of the hedge, nor a dear friend on the hill; but the two lines take you with Tao into a sphere beyond the reach of the worries and cares of the world. Or listen to Wang Wei of the same land:

> "Softly I harp and sing alone,
>   In the quietude of wooded bamboo;
> Not a soul into deep solitude, but the
>   Telltale moon comes, and speaks its
>   heart."

A world looms up from the four verses, the charm of which is not that of popular novels, but a good you feel from a sound and all-forgetting sleep you have had, after being thoroughly tired of steamers, railways, rights and duties, morals and formalities. Sleep? Yes, and if sleep be necessary even in the Twentieth century, equally indispensable to the Twentieth century is this super-earthly poetical sentiment. Unfortunately poetry makers and poetry readers are nowadays all enamoured of the Westerners, and none seem to care to take a boat and float to the land of the immortals. I am not a poet by profession, and am interested in no way whatever in spreading propaganda for the kind of life led by Wang

Wei and Tao Yuan-ming, in the present world. Only to me it appears that such inspired feelings as are sung by the Chinese poets are more powerful in remedying the ills and evils of the day than theatricals and dancing parties. They are, at all events far more agreeable to me than *Faust* or *Hamlet*. I come into the mountain with a colour-box and a tripod for my sole companions, all because I yearn to drink direct from nature of the poetical wine of Tao Yuan-ming and Wang Wei; to be away from the world-smelling and world-sounding world, nay, to breathe and live in an unhuman atmosphere, even for a brief while. It is a weakness of mine if you like to call it so.

I am at any rate, a living block of humanity, and however fond I may be of unhumanity, my love of it cannot go so very far. I do not suppose that even Tao Yuan-ming had his eye on the Southern hill, year in and year out; nor is it imaginable that Wang Wei slept in his bamboo jungle without a mosquito net. In all likelihood Tao sold his chrysanthemums to a florist after keeping what he wanted, and Wang his bamboo sprouts to a greengrocer. I myself am not unhuman enough to live under the blue sky in the mountain, just because the lark and golden rape captivate my fancy. Such as the place is, human beings are not a rarity—men with their heads wrapped in a towel and their kimono tucked up at the back; country lasses in red skirts and so on, and sometimes also even long faced horses. Breathing the mountain air, hundreds of feet above the sea level, surrounded by a million cypresses, I could not still be rid of human smell. Nay, I was crossing the mountain to reach the hot spring hotel of Nakoi as my destination for the night.

However, things assume shapes or colour as you will, according to the way you look at them. In the words of Leonardo Da Vinci to a pupil of his "the bell is one; but listen, and its sound may be heard in all sorts of ways." Opinions may differ in a man or a woman, all depending upon how you look at him or her. I had come out in my present tour to indulge in unhumanity and people would appear different from what they did when I was living round the corner in the crowded Mud-and-Dust Lane, if I looked at them now, I thought, bearing in mind my unhumanity idea. Impossible as entirely getting away from humanity may be, I should be able to bring myself up or down to suit the frame of mind, in which one finds oneself at a Noh[1] play. The Noh has its humanity or sentimental side. Who can be sure not to be moved to tears by the *Shichikiochi* or by the *Sumidagawa*? But the Noh performance is seven-tenth art and three-tenth sentiment. The attractions of Noh do not come from the lifelike presentation of things human in this mundane world; because the lifelike in it appears only from under many, many layers of art, which give it an air of extreme tranquility and halcyon serenity, never to be met in the world of reality.

How would it do to interpret all the events and people I came across in the present tour as part of performances on the Noh stage? I could not cast aside humanity altogether. To be poetical at the bottom of my whole venture, I should like to let unhumanity carry me into a Noh atmosphere, by doing away with humanity as much as possible. Different in nature from the "Southern hill" or the "bamboo grove," nor identifiable with the lark or blossoming rapes, I still would see people from a point of view as near those objects as possible. The man Basho[2] saw something poetical and made a hokku[3] even of a horse stalling near his head! I would deal with everybody I was going to meet—farmers, tradesmen, the village offce clerk, old men, old women—seeing in them only objects, complementing a picture. However unlike figures on the canvas, they would move as they please. It would be grossly common, however, to enquire, as does an ordinary novelist, into the cause of each of them going his own way, to dig into their mental state, or to try to solve the tangle of their human affairs. I shall not care, move as they will. They won't trouble me, as I shall regard them as characters in a picture in motion. Painted figures cannot get out of the plane of the picture, no matter how they may move. Troubles would arise of conflicting views and clash of interests, the moment you think, the characters might jump out of the plane and act cubically. The more troublesome the matter grew, the more impossible it would become to look at it aesthetically. Wherever I might go and whomever I might meet, I should look at them as from a transcendental height, so that human-magnetism might not easily pass between us, and I shall, then, be not easily affected, however animatedly they might act. In short I am to assume the position of one standing before a picture, and looking at the figures in it, running hither and thither on its plane. With three feet between, you can calmly look on, without any sense of danger. In other words, you run no risk of anybody snatching away your weapon and you may give yourself up altogether to studying their doings from an artistic point of view. With undivided attention you may see and judge the objects before you as beautiful or as not beautiful.

By the time I had come to this decision, the sky began to assume a doubtful aspect. A bank of clouds of indistinct foreboding had no sooner mounted overhead than it went tumbling and overspreading until the whole space seemed to turn into a hanging expanse of dark sea. From the sea soft Spring rain began to fall. I had long since gone past the golden rape blossoms and was now toiling along between two mountains; but the threads of rain being so fine as to appear as mist, I could not tell how distant they were. Now and again, as the gusts of wind blew asunder the high drapery of cloud, a grey ridge of mountain showed itself to the right as clearly as within reach of a hand: probably the range ran on the other side of the valley. The left side seemed to be the foot of another mountain. Back of the semitransparent screen of rain, trees—they might be pines—appeared and then disappeared, with an endless frequency. Was it the rain that was moving? Or was it the trees in motion? Could it be that I was dreaming a floating dream? I trudged on, feeling strange.

The road became wider than I had imagined, and quite level also. Walking was no longer a task; but being not prepared for rain, I had to hurry.

About the time the rainwater began to fall in drops from my hat, I heard a jingle, jingle of a bell some yards away, and there appeared a packhorse driver leading an animal behind him.

"Hello, any place to stop around here, man?"

"A mile more or so, you will come upon a tea stall. Getting pretty wet, eh?"

A mile more! The figure of the rustic dissolved into rain like a magic lantern view, as I looked back.

The misty rain had now become thick and long until each drop could be seen distinctly like a pencil flying in the wind. It had long since soaked through my outer garment, and then penetrated to the skin. The heat of my body made lukewarm the water in my underwear and the feeling produced was by no means the most pleasant. I pulled my hat to one side and quickened my pace.

The drenching figure of myself, running through a grey expanse of space, with innumerable silver shafts beating at it slantingly will make poetry, an ode, when I look at it as not my own. I make a beautiful harmony with a natural scenery, as a figure in a picture, when I forget my material self completely and take a purely objective view of myself. Only, I cease to be a figure in poetry, or in a picture, the moment I feel vexed with the falling rain and take to heart the tiredness of the stamp, stamp of my feet. I then find myself only an indifferent individual of the street, blind to the changing humour of the flying clouds; untouched by the falling flowers, and the carols of birds; nay, a perfect stranger to the beauty of my own self going alone and quietly through a mountain in Spring. I walked first with my hat pulled to one side; but later I kept my eyes pivoted on the back of my feet. Finally I went gingerly, shrugging my shoulders. The rain shook the tree tops all round, and closed in from all sides upon a lonely traveller. I felt I was having rather too strong a dose of unhumanity.

II

"Are you there?" I said, but no response came.

I was standing before the humblest shop, which had at its rear papered sliding screens, shutting from view a room behind. A bunch of straw sandals for sale was hanging from the eve, swinging forlornly. Under a low counter were a few trays of cheap sweets, with some small coins lying about.

"Are you there?" I said again. The ejaculation startled, this time, a hen and her lord, which awoke clucking on a mortar, on which they had been standing bulged and asleep. I was glad to find fire going in a clay furnace, part of which had its colour changed by the rain that had been falling a minute ago. A teakettle was hanging from a suspender over the furnace. It was black with smoke, too black, indeed, to tell whether it was earthen or silver.

Receiving no answer, I took the liberty of walking into the shop and sitting on a bench before the fire, and this made the fowls flap their wings and hop from the mortar onto the raised and matted floor and they would have gone through the inner room had it not been for the screens. The birds clucked and cackled in alarm as if they thought I were a fox or a cur.

Presently footsteps were heard, a paper screen slid open, and out came an old woman, as I knew somebody would, with a fire going, and money lying scattered about. This was somewhat different from the city, that a woman could, with no concern, be away, leaving her shop to take care of itself and it was at any rate, unlike the twentieth century, that I could go into the shop and sit on a bench uninvited to wait, wait and wait. All this "unhuman" condition of things delighted me immensely. What charmed me most was, however, the look of the aged shopkeeper who had come out.

I discovered in her, living, the aged, masked dame of Takasago whom I saw at the Hosho Noh theatre, two or three years ago. I snapped that dame's image into my mind's camera at the time as most fascinating, wondering how an old woman could look so gentle and reverentially attractive. I say, I saw in flesh and blood this Noh figure in the lowly shopkeeper bowing before me. In response to my apologetic remark that I had taken possession of her bench in her absence, she said very civilly:

"I did not know that you had come in, *Danna-sama*."[4]

"Had been raining rather hard?"

"Bad weather, *Danna-sama*, you must have had a hard time of it. Why you are drenching wet. Wait, I will make a big fire and let you dry yourself."

"Thank you. Put just a little more wood there, and I shall warm and dry myself. The rest has made me feel cold."

We kept on talking about the quietness of the place, the *uguisu*,[5] and so on. Out came my sketch book, and I made a hasty picture of the old woman, as she worked at the fire. The rain had stopped, and the sky cleared up. I saw the "Hobgoblin Cliff" by turning my eyes in the direction towards which my good woman pointed. I glanced at the cliff and then at the woman, and last of all I looked at them both half and half. Of the impressions of old women carved permanently in my head, there were that of the face of the Takasago dame of the Noh mask, and that of the she-spirit of the mountain drawn by Rosetsu. The Rosetsu picture has made me think that an ideal old woman is a weird creature and that she should be seen only among autumn tinted trees or else in cold moonlight. But on seeing the mask of the Takasago dame I was astonished at the extent to which the aged of the other sex could be made to look so sweet. I have since thought she could, with her warm and graceful expression, ornament a golden screen, be a figure in a balmy Spring breeze or that she could go well, even with cherry blossoms. As I looked at my homely dressed hostess of motherly kindness, with a beaming light on her face, I fancied she made a picture better in keeping with the Spring scenery of the mountain, than with the "Hobgoblin Cliff," she was pointing at, with one hand shading her eyes. I had almost finished sketching her when her pose broke. It was disconcerting, and with chagrin I held my book to the fire to dry.

"You look hale and hearty, *O-Bah-san*."[6]

"Yes, thank you, *Danna-sama*. I can sew; I can spin hemp."

She added triumphantly, "I can grind rice for dumpling flour!" I felt I would like to see her work at the mill stones. However such a request was out of place, and I changed the topic of conversation by asking her if it was not more than two and a half miles to Nakoi.

"No, *Danna-sama*, about two miles they say. You are going to the hot spring there, then?"

"I may stop there a while, if the place is not crowded. Or rather I should say if I am in the mood."

"No crowding, I am sure, *Danna-sama*. The place has been almost deserted since the war (Russo-Japanese) broke out. The spa hostelry is all but closed."

"Well, well. They won't let me stop there then."

"Oh, yes, they will any time, *Danna-sama*, if you just ask them."

"There is only one hotel there; isn't that so?"

"Yes, *Danna-sama*, ask for Shiota and anybody will tell you. Squire Shiota is a rich man of the village and one doesn't know to call the place which, a hot-spring resort or the old gentleman's pleasure retreat."

"Is that so? Guest or no guest makes no difference to him then?"

"*Danna-sama* is going there for the first time?"

"No, not quite. I was there once long ago."

There came a temporary lull in our conversation, here, as if by mutual agreement. In the silence that followed, I once more took out my sketch book and began to make a picture of the rooster and his mate, when the jingling of bells caught my ear, the sound making a music of its own in my head. I felt as if I were listening, in a dream, to a mortar-and-pestle rhythm coming from a neighbour's. I stopped sketching and wrote down instead:

"Harukazeya Inen-ga mimini[7]
Umano Suzu."[8]

Coming up the mountain, I passed five or six pack horses and found them all wearing aprons between their fore and hind legs, with bells jingling about their necks. I could not help imagining I was encountering in spirit ghosts long past. Presently there rose above the jingling of bells a quaintly long drawn note of *mago-uta,*[9] floating dreamily in the peaceful Spring air of the mountain, and gradually coming upward. This made my rustic but gentle hostess say, as if speaking to herself: "Somebody is coming again."

Every passer, coming and going seemed to be the good woman's acquaintance, since the pass lay in a single line, and all traffic must go by the humble tea-stall. All of the half-dozen drivers of packhorses, I met on the road, must have come up or gone down the mountain, everyone of them making her think somebody was coming. I could not help wondering how often, indeed, times out of number, her ears must have caught the jingling of bells in the years past, that had turned her hair so completely grey. Oh, how long she must have lived in this little place with its lonely road, where spring had come and gone, gone and come, with no ground to walk on, lest one crushed little flowers under foot! I wrote down another haiku in my book:

"Mago-utaya Shiragamo

Somede Kururu Haru"[10]

The little verse did not quite express my poetical fancy, and I was gazing at the point of my pencil to compress into seventeen syllables the ideas of grey hair, and the cycles of years as well as the quaint tunes of a country packhorse driver, and departing Spring, when a live bucolic individual, leading a pony, halted before the shop and greeted the old woman:

"Good day, *Oba-san*!"[11]

"Why, it is you Gen-san. You are going down to the town?"

"I am, and shall be glad to get, if there be anything you want down there."

"Let me see. Stop at my daughter's, if you happen to go along Kajicho, and ask her to get for me a holy tablet of the Reiganji temple."

"All right, only one, eh? Your O-Aki-san[12] is very lucky that she has been so well married, don't you think so, *Oba-san*?"

"I am thankful that she is not in want of daily needs. Maybe she is happy."

"Of course she is. Look at that *Jo-sama*[13] of Nakoi!"

"Poor *O-Jo-sama*, my heart aches for her and she is so beautiful. Is she any better these days?"

"No, the same as ever."

"Too bad," sighs mine hostess, and "Yes, too bad" assents Gen-san, patting his horse on the head. A gust of wind came just then and shook a cherry tree outside and the raindrops lodging precariously among its leaves and flowers shed like a fresh shower, making the horse toss his long mane up and down with a start. I had by this time fallen into a train of fancy from which I was awakened by Gen-san's "Whoa" and the jingling of the horse's bells, to hear the *Oba-san* say:

"Ah, I still see before me the *Jo-sama* in her bridal dress with her hair done up in a high *Shimada* style and going horseback...."

"Yes, yes, she went on horseback, not by boat. We stopped here, didn't we, *Oba-san*?"

"Aye, when the *Jo-sama's* horse stopped under that cherry tree, a falling petal alighted on her hair, dressed so carefully."

The old woman's word-sketch was fascinating, well worthy of a picture; of poetry. A vision of a charming bride came before my mind's eye, and musing on the scene described, I wrote down in my sketch book:

> *"Hanano Koro-o Koete*
> *Kashikoshi Umani Yome."*[14]

I had a clear vision of the girl's hair and dress, the horse and the cherry tree; but strangely enough, her face would not come to me, eagerly as my fancy travelled from one type to another. Suddenly Millais' *Ophelia* came into the vision under the bride's *shimada* coiffure. No good, I thought and let my vision crumble away. The same moment the bridal dress, hair, horse, and cherry tree and all disappeared from my mind's setting; but Ophelia floating above the water with her hands clasped, remained behind mistily in my mind, lingering with a faintness, as of a cloud of smoke brushed with a palm fibre whisk, and producing a weird sensation as when looking at the fading tail of a shooting star.

"Well, goodbye *Oba-san*."

"Come again on your way back. Bad time we had with the rain. The road must be pretty bad about the 'Seven Bends.'"

Gen-san began to move and his horse to trot as he said: "rather a job," leaving behind the jingling of bells.

"Was that man from Nakoi?"

"Yes, he is Gembei of Nakoi."

"Do I understand that that man crossed this mountain with a bride on the back of his horse, some time or other?"

"He passed here with the *Jo-sama* of Nakoi on the back of his horse, when the ladybird went to her future husband's house.—Time goes fast; it was five years ago."

She is of a happy order, who laments the turning white of her hair only when she looks into the glass. Nearer an immortal, I thought, was my old woman who became conscious of the swiftness of fleeting time only by counting five years on her fingers. I observed to her:

"She must have been charming.—I wish I was here to see her."

"Haw, haw, but you may see her. She will come out, I am sure, to receive you, if you put up at the hot-spring hotel of Nakoi."

"Why, then, is she back in her father's house, now? I wonder if I could see her in her bridal dress, with her hair done up in the *shimada*."

"Only ask her; she will most likely oblige you by appearing in the dress of her bridal tour."

Impossible! I thought, but my *bah-san*[15] was quite in earnest. After all, my "unhuman" tour would be insipid, if it were all commonplace with no such characters. My good woman went on:

"There is so much alike between the *Jo-sama* and Nagarano Otome."

"You mean in their looks?"

"No, I mean in their life."

"But who is this Nagarano Otome?"

"Long, long ago, there was the maid of Nagara, the beautiful daughter of a rich man, and the pride of this village."

"Yes?"

"Well, *Danna-sama*, two men, Sasada-otoko and Sasabe-otoko fell in love with her both at once."

"I see."

"Shall she accept the hand of the Sasada man or should give her heart to the Sasabe man? She tormented herself for days, weeks, and months, with the perplexing problem, until unable to allow herself the choice of one in preference to the other, she ended her life by throwing herself into a river, leaving behind her an ode:

> *"Akizukeba Obanaga Uyeni*
> *Okutsuyuno*
> *Kenubekumo Wawa*
> *Omohoyurukana."*[16]

I had little expected to hear such a quaint romance told in such old-fashioned language, least of all from such an old woman in the depth of a mountain like this.

"You go down about 600 yards East from here *Danna-sama* and you will come upon the 'five elements' spiral tombstone on the roadside, that marks the eternal home of Nagarano Otome. You should pay a visit to the grave, on your way to Nakoi."

I resolved by all means to see the grave. The *Bah-san* went on to tell me:

"The *Jo-sama* of Nakoi had, in her evil days, her hand sought by two suitors. One of them was a young man she met while she was at school in Kyoto, and the other a son of the wealthiest man in the castled town."

"So? Which did she choose?"

"The *Jo-sama* herself would have had her lover in Kyoto if she could make her own choice; but her father forced her to accept the young man of the castled-town."

"That is to say, she fortunately escaped drowning herself in the river?"

"To her young husband she was as dear as his own life, and he did all he could to please her; but she was not happy to the worry of all. Soon after the present war had broken out her husband lost his job, the bank where he was working closing its doors, while the same cause wrought the ruin of his own family. This made the *Jo-sama* come back to her father's house in Nakoi, and gossip has been busy making a heartless and ungrateful woman of her. As a girl, the *Jo-sama* was always coy and gentle; but she has latterly been changing into a woman of unwomanly high spirits. So says Gembey every time he passes here, as he feels really sorry for her."

I did not want to hear more, to have my fancies spoiled. The woman's story was beginning to smell of human ills and worries and I felt as if somebody was wanting back the fairy wand, when I was just becoming celestial. It cost me uncommon pains to negotiate the perils of the "Seven Bends," and reach here. All that and the very reason of my wandering out of my house would have been lost, if I were now to be so recklessly brought back to the everyday world. This and that of life are all very well up to a certain point; but past that limit it brings a worldly odor that enters you through the pores of the skin and makes you feel heavy with dirt. So I started to go, with this departing word, after depositing a silver piece on the bench: "The road is straight to Nakoi, is it not *O-bah-san*?"

"Turn right, down the slope from the tomb of Nagarano Otome and you will make a saving of some half a mile. The road is not very good; but a young gentleman like you would make a shortcut.... God bless you for such generosity. Take good care of yourself, *Danna-sama*."

III

I had a queer time of it last night.

About eight o'clock I reached the hotel. It had already closed up for the night, and was but dimly lighted. I could not, of course, tell, then, the plan of the house or the layout of its garden, to say nothing of its bearing on the points of the compass. I was led by the nose, as it were, through a long, long winding sort of passage, at the end of which I was put in a small room of about six mats. I could not at all tell where I was; the place had so completely changed since I was here last. After supper, and then a dip in the hot spring bath, I was sipping tea in my room, when a young girl came in, and asked me if she should make my bed.

What struck me as not a little strange was that it was the same girl who had come out to let me in when I arrived; it was this same girl who had brought me supper and waited on me; it was this same girl who had showed me to the bath room; and it was again this same girl who took upon herself the trouble of making the bed for me. This little woman seemed to have everything on her shoulders in this establishment; and yet she seldom spoke a word. I would have done her injustice, however, if I said she was country-looking. When she went before me, with her girlish crimson obi[17] tied unsentimentally on her back, and with an old-fashioned burning candle in her hand, taking me round and round along a corridor-like and stairway-like passages, when she with the same crimson obi and the same candlestick, led me down places, of which it was difficult to say whether they were corridors or staircases, down to the bath tank, I felt as if I were myself a figure in a picture moving in a world of canvas.

When she waited on me at supper, she begged me to put up with the room I was in, which was, she said, one of family use, as the other rooms were undusted, no guests coming these days. When she finished making my bed she spoke humanly, wishing me "a good night of rest," before she left my room. My ears followed her footsteps along the long wriggling sort of passage until they finally died out far away. Then stillness fell and the whole place seemed to have become deserted by all things human.

Only once before in all my life, I went through an experience like this. Long ago I crossed Boshu from Tateyama to the Pacific sea coast, and went on foot from Kazusa to Choshi along the sea shore. On the way I stopped overnight at a place. At a place, and I cannot say less vaguely as the name of the locality and of the inn where I lodged had both long since been forgotten. It is not even clear that it was really an inn where I passed the night. The house was very large but inhabited by only two women. I asked them if they would let me stop overnight. The older of the two said "yes" and the younger said: "This way please." I followed the latter past many spacious but deserted and neglected rooms, and was finally shown up the innermost semi-two-storey flat. I mounted three staircases and was about to enter my room, when a gust of evening wind made a bunch of bamboos, growing bendingly under the eve, rustle against my head and shoulders, somehow chilling me to the bones. The wooden flooring of the verandah, I stepped upon, was almost crumbling with age. I remarked, then, the sprouts would pierce through the flooring and take possession of the room next spring. The young woman said nothing but went away grinning.

That night, the rustling of bamboos robbed me of all my sleep. I slid open the front paper screen and found myself looking over, in the clear Summer moonlight, a grass-grown garden, which had no boundary hedge or fence, but stretched into a weedy elevation, beyond which the great ocean roared with its tumbling breakers, menacing the world of man. I passed the whole night nervously awake, imprisoning myself in an apology of a mosquito net. My lot that night might be, I thought, a page from some weird story book.

I had never since felt as I did then, until my first night at Nakoi.

I was lying on my back in my bed, and my eyes accidentally caught sight of some Chinese writing mounted in a vermilion frame, hung high up a wall. It consisted of seven big characters which said: "Shadow of bamboos sweeping no dust rises." It was signed "Daitetsu." Then my fancy travelled for a while into the realm of autographs. A Jakuchu in the picture hanging niche next entered my eyes. It was a picture of a crane standing on one foot, a production of a bold sweep of brush, that pleased me marvellously. In a little while I fell asleep and was soon lost in dreamland.

The Maiden of Nagara appeared before me, in a long-sleeved bridal gown, crossing a mountain on a pony. The Sasabe Otoko and the Sasada Otoko suddenly slipped into the scene, and began struggling to carry away the maiden. Thereupon the girl changed as suddenly into Ophelia, mounting a branch of willow tree, and then floating down a stream. She was singing sweetly. Eager to rescue her, I reached a long pole and ran along Mukojima with it. She showed no sign of struggle, but was smiling and singing as the tide carried her down, down to where I knew not. I hallooed and hallooed to her, with the pole on my shoulder.

My hallooing awoke me. I was wet with perspiration. What a curious mixture of the poetical and vulgar, I thought. Priest Ta Hui in the Sung days of China, who claimed to be able to have everything his way after he had attained his Buddhistic emancipation, complained that he was nevertheless vulnerable to unworthy thoughts that cropped up in his dreams. He is said to have suffered long and greatly from this failing. I thought that was quite natural. It would do little credit to anyone making art one's life to dream a not more beautiful dream. One such as I dreamed would in greater part make neither a picture nor poetry worthy of the name. Thinking thus, I turned my body over in bed and saw the moon shining on the paper screen, casting on it the shadow of some branches of tree. The night looked almost bright.

Possibly just a fancy; but I thought I heard someone singing or rather chanting softly. I pricked my ears to know if it was a song that had escaped from dreamland into this world of reality, or a real voice flowing into dreams? I was sure there was someone singing. The voice was indisputably thin and low; but faint as it was, it was pulsating the Spring night, which was on the verge of sleep. The weird part of it was that, whatever its tune, its wording, of which there was no reason that it could be heard clearly, being not uttered near me, nevertheless came distinctly, the sinking voice repeating over and over the song of Nagarano Otome: "Even like the dew drop, that when autumn comes, lodges on grass leaves, must I roll off to die."

The chanting sounded first near the verandah; but it gradually grew fainter and farther. What ceases suddenly produces a feeling of suddenness; but it leaves little room for sentiment. A voice that speaks peremptorily resolution rouses also a feeling of peremptoriness and resolution in others. But confronted by a phenomenon that had no definite limit but went on thinning and thinning until it would imperceptibly disappear altogether, you could not help feeling that you must mince up the minute and split the second, your sense of helplessness and hopelessness momentarily deepening. The chant sounded dying like a dying man, becoming more and more feeble like an outgoing light; and in that song that distracted the heart as if with the approaching end, there was a tune that spoke for all the sorrows of the Spring of the whole world.

I listened to the song, holding myself down in the bed; but as it went farther and farther, I felt, I must chase it, despite the consciousness that it was luring me out by the ear. The thinner it grew the more I felt that I should let my ear only fly after it. Just at the moment I thought, however hard I might listen, my ears would hear no more, I could constrain myself no longer and unconsciously I slipped out of my bed. The same moment I opened the shoji,[18] and stood out in the verandah, with the lower half of my body bathing in the moonlight and a tree throwing its waving shadow on my night clothes. These details did not occur to me, however, at the instant I opened the shoji.

But that dying sound? I looked in the direction toward which my ear was running. There I espied a shadowy form in the moonlight as it were, with its back to a tree, which, if in bloom, might be an aronia. The misty dark thing flanked right, stepping on the shadow of blossoms on the ground, even before it had left on me a clear impression that "it must be it." A corner of the roof, thrown on the ground, of a room adjoining mine, seemed to move lithely, and the next moment shut out from view a tall figure of a woman.

I was lost to myself for many moments, as I stood thinly clad in my night gown, with my hand on the screen. The minute I returned to myself, I was made keenly conscious that a night of Spring in the mountain was decidedly chilly. As it was, I did not hesitate to permit myself to creep back into the bed from which I had crept out, and started on another train of thought. I took out my watch from under the pillow and found it pointing at ten past one. I put the watch back under the pillow, and returned to my thoughts. "It cannot be a spook," I thought. If not an apparition, it must be a human being, and if a human being, it must be a woman. She might have been the *O-Jo-san* of this house. If so, it seemed rather defying propriety that a young woman, who had taken a divorce of her husband should, at that hour of night, be out in the garden, that ran into the mountain. In any case, sleep had become impossible, that watch of mine under the pillow ticking me to irrepressible wakefulness. The tiny ticking of my watch had never before troubled me; but on this particular night it seemed to say "No sleep for you tonight, but think, think, think." It was outrageously extraordinary.

A frightful thing will make poetry when you regard it merely as the form itself of frightfulness; just as a weird eerie sight may be worked into a picture, if you treat it as something horrid in itself, independent of you. Likewise a disappointed love makes an excellent theme of art when gentleness, sympathy, worries and, indeed, even the very overflow of pains, it occasions, are turned objectively into visions before you, divorced from the actual torments felt in your heart. Nay, some people imagine that they are disappointed in love in order to enjoy the pleasure of agonising themselves. Ordinary mortals laugh at them as idiotic, as lunatic; but they are no more unbalanced, from the point of view of having their own artistic ground to stand on, than those who go into the ecstacy of living in a world of their own by creating scenery that nowhere exists.

Looked at in this light, artists as such are, compared with common people, idiots, lunatics—whatever be their qualification in their daily life. When by themselves they never cease complaining, from morn till night, of the hardships of their pedestrian journeys in search of fit subjects for their canvas or for their pen. But they betray not even a shadow of grievance when they tell others of their experiences. They not only narrate gleefully the things they enjoyed and were delighted with, but are enthusiastic over events that once tortured them but now come back as sweet memories. Not that they mean to deceive themselves and others; but the truth is that when out on the road they see and feel as ordinary mortals do, but they become poets when they talk of their past. And this accounts for their inconsistencies. He may be called an artist, then, who lives in a triangle, built by knocking off a corner called common sense of the four-angled world.

Be it in nature or in the world of man, artists thus discover countless gems and stones of inestimable value, in places which the multitude dare not approach. The secret of such a discovery is commonly called beautifying. But in reality there is no beautification about it at all, light and colour having in their brilliancy always existed in this mundane world; but because flowers fall from the sky in vain for common eyes; because worldly trammels are unshakable; because the thought of success and prosperity hang so heavy on the human mind, nobody has been able to see the beauties of a railway train till Turner showed them, and the world waited for Ohkyo to be shown the aesthetics of a ghost.

The shadow I had just seen had, as a phenomenon complete in itself and nothing more, something poetical about it that none could deny who saw or heard it. A sequestered spa in the bosom of a mountain—the shadow of flowers in a Spring night—The soft warbling of a song under a telltale moon—a dreamy figure in pale moonlight—every one of them would have made a capital subject for an artist. For all that, I was trying unnecessarily to see what might be behind the vision, and a blood-chilling sensation that had taken possession of me blinded me to the elegance of the situation, which was perfectly consistent in itself and the picturesqueness that could not be hoped for. I thought myself unworthy of my professed unhumanity and felt I must go through more training before I could proclaim myself a poet or an artist. Salvator Rosa of Italy came vividly before my eyes with his perilous tale of joining the banditti of the Abruzzi. I had wandered away from my home with just a sketch book, and I should be ashamed of myself, if I had not Rosa's resolve.

How should I rehabilitate myself as a poet in such circumstances? All that is necessary is, I argued to myself, I may put myself in a condition that would enable me to take hold of my feelings, lay them before me, stand a step behind, and examine them calmly unprejudicedly as if I were another person, not myself. The poet is under an obligation, when he dies, to dissect his own body and publish the cause of his malady. There may be various ways of doing this; but the easiest and nearest is to make an instantaneous survey of everything you can lay your hand on, and reduce it into a seventeen syllable hokku. The seventeen syllable effusion is the simplest of poems, and you can have it, when you are washing your face in the morning, or when you are going in a tram car. It makes a poet of you most simply and most easily. To be a poet is to be enlightened, and I mean no disparagement, when I say, it is the simplest and easiest. The simpler the more beneficial it is, and should the more be respected. Suppose you lose your temper. You make a seventeen syllable hokku of your indignation. The moment seventeen syllables get into shape, your anger becomes something outside of you—you cannot be fuming with anger and composing a hokku at the same time. You are moved to tears; you make seventeen syllables, and they delight you. When your tears are changed into seventeen syllables, your tearful anguish has left you, and you have become a self only joyous of being a man capable of weeping.

This has always been the stand I insisted upon, and I now wanted to put it to a practical test. Lying abed, I set about making a series of seventeen syllables of the events of the night. A very deliberate enterprise as I was undertaking, I lay open my sketchbook near the pillow, to jot down in it as fast as I got the lines, lest they might become lost as fugitive thoughts, hard to recapture.

"*Kaidono tsuyuo furu-u-ya monogurui,*"[19] I wrote down as my first production. If the reading of it did not strike me as particularly captivating, neither did it give rise to any uncomfortably creepy feeling. I next jotted down: "*Hanano kage, onnano kageno oborokana.*"[20] It was faulty with a redundancy. I forgave myself for it; because all I wanted was to recover calmness and humour myself into an easy frame of mind. For the third piece, I ventured: "*Shoichi-i onnani bakete oborozuki.*"[21] It sounded droll and amused me.

All was right at this rate, I thought, and getting into the spirit of the thing, I scribbled down all that follow, one after another:

*"Haruno hoshio otoshite
     Yowano kazashikana."*[22]

*"Haruno yono kumoni
     Nurasuya araigami."*[23]

*"Haruya koyoi
     Uta tsukamatsuru onsugata."*[24]

*"Kaido no seiga
     Detekuru tsukiyokana."*[25]

*"Uta oriori gekkano
     Haruo ochikochisu."*[26]

*"Omoi kitte fukeyuku
     Haruno hitorikana."*[27]

Sleep was stealing over me by the time I had finished committing the last piece to the sketchbook.

I was half asleep and half awake, in a condition, to describe which was invented, I thought, the expression "as in a trance." Nobody is conscious of self in a sound sleep; but in wakefulness the world outside is never forgotten. Between the two regions lies the borderland of vision, where things look too misty to be called awake, and yet too animate to be in sleep. It is a condition in which "up awake" and "lie asleep" are put in one and the same cup and stirred and mixed up with the straw of poetry and song. Shade off the colours of nature into all but a dream, push this universe of reality adrift into the sea of haze, and smooth into curves all sharp angles with the magic hand of the genie of sleep. Breathe slow pulsation into the world so tempered. Imagine clouds of smoke crawling the surface of such a world, unable to fly away though it would; imagine again your soul about to depart lingering, unable to leave its shell. Such is the condition I mean. It is again the state in which the soul is lambently struggling, and finally unable to preserve its entity dissolves into an ethereal existence and clings and hangs about with no heart to depart.

I was traversing this borderland of dreamy consciousness when the *karakami*[28] of my room opened, as if of its own accord, and in the opening appeared the figure of a woman, like a phantom. The apparition did not cause me surprise, nor did it frighten me: I simply looked at it with easy pleasant sensation. Perhaps I put it too strongly to say I "looked at"; for the truth was, the shadowy thing slid with no permission of mine behind the lids of my eyes, which were closed. The phantom slowly came into my room, with the smoothness of a fairy queen walking across a placid surface of water. The matted floor gave no sound of human footsteps. I could not tell distinctly as I was looking through closed eyelids; but she looked fair, with a wealth of hair and a long well-shaped neck, making me feel as if I were throwing my eyes on a vignette of latter-day vogue, held up against a light.

The vision stopped before a cupboard in the rear of the room. A *karakami* screening the cupboard was pushed open and a slim arm visible in the dark came out of a sleeve. The screen closed then and the phantom sailed noiselessly back to the opening, which, in the next moment, closed of itself. Sleep now gathered faster and faster on me. The dead must feel as I did then, I obscurely imagined, before being reborn into a horse or an ox.

I did not know how long I had been wandering between man and horse; only I opened my eyes. The curtain of night had apparently been raised long since, and the world was light from end to end, with the bright Spring sun printing darkly bamboo lattices on the window shoji,[29] leaving no room, as it appeared, for any spooky things to lurk about on the face of the earth. The mysterious apparition must have hied into the far, far away world on the other side of the Styx.

I went straightway down to the bathroom for a morning dip. I just held my head above water for a full five minutes, perfectly will-less to wash my face or to be getting out. How could I have gone, I wondered, into such state of mind as I did last night and how could the world go head-over-heels so completely by merely crossing the boundary line of night and day.

I was too lazy to dry myself and was coming out of the bathroom almost wet, when to my surprise, simultaneous with my opening the bathroom door from within, a voice—that of a woman—outside said: "Good morning, did you sleep well last night?"

I had expected no one on the other side of the door, and the greeting came with such absolute suddenness that I was at a loss for an answer. The voice then said: "Put this on and be good; so there." This was said as the person, from whom the voice proceeded, went behind me and put gently on my back a kimono deliciously soft to the skin,[32] Then and only then did the command of words return to me sufficiently to enable me to blurt out: "So kind of you, thank you." The woman withdrew a step or two backward as I turned to say this.

Now, it is an unwritten law for novelists, from time immemorial, to give the minutest portrayal of their hero or heroine. If words, phrases, clauses, and effusions employed by ancients as well as by moderns, of the East and of the West, in describing and speaking of beautiful women, were collected, they might, indeed, out-volume even the great Buddhist Sutras. The words might mount up to a countless number, if I were to pick out, from this overwhelming accumulation of adjectives, those that would fit the woman, who was standing three steps from me, with her body slightly twisted halfway round toward me and looking at me from the corner of her eyes, as if enjoying my amazement and embarrassment. To confess the truth, I had never yet seen an expression like this woman's in the thirty years of my life. According to the Greek sculptural ideals, the artists say, calmness seems to be that state of force in which it is ready for, but has not yet gone, into action. Roused into action it may awake the winds and clouds and bring down a thunderstorm. But one does not know what, and it is precisely the consciousness of this profound and unseen potentiality that makes the Greek art live for centuries and centuries with its unchanging powers of fascination. This serene calmness with its electric possibilities, it is which forms the source of what the world calls dignity and augustness. But once in motion the force must take one form or another, and once in form it can no longer retain its mystic powers, nor can it recover its perfection. There is always, thus, something low and mean in motion. This one word motion, it was, that made failures of Unkey's *Niwo* and Hokusai's comic pictures. Motion or rest? That is where the vital question hangs for us artists. The qualities of beautiful women, from the oldest of times, may be brought under either one of these categories.

But the woman before me was a puzzle, her expression defying my power of judgment. Her lips were tightly sealed, and yet they seemed to speak. Her eyes were ceaselessly on the alert, indeed, motion itself. Her face was a lovely oval, somewhat fleshy downward and altogether calmly composed. Her brow was narrow, not quite in keeping with her generally classical features. Especially noticeable were her eyebrows that almost joined, and the nervous twitching going on between them as if a drop of mint oil were drying there. Not so with her nose, which was neither too thin and sharp, bespeaking flippancy nor beetle-like, indicating dullness, but was of such shape as would make a fine picture. In short, her features, taken separately, had each its own point of significance, and it was no wonder I was at a loss as they all at once crowded into my eyes with no claim to harmony.

Supposing an earthquake occurred, convulsing the earth. Suppose that awakening to the fact that motion is against one's nature, one strives to recover one's former repose; but carried by the force of lost balance, one keeps on in motion, in spite of oneself, and wants in desperation to be now agitated with a vengeance. Suppose one is capable of an expression reflecting such a state of things, then it was precisely such an expression that I saw in the woman before me.

Thus it was that behind her look of contempt, I could see a flicker of yearning, and the gleam of a careful mind from under a mocking air. She looked as if she thought nothing of a hundred men, when she let loose her wit and rode on her high spirits. There was no unity of expression. I might have said, light and darkness of mind were living under the same roof, quarreling. The fact that there was no unity in her expression was evidence, as I took it, that there was no unity in her mind. That there was no unity in her mind must be the consequence of there being no unity in the world in which she had lived. Hers was the face of one struggling to overcome the unhappiness that was weighing down upon her. She must be a woman standing under a star of ill-luck.

"Thank you." Repeating the words, I lightly bowed to her.

"Your room is dusted. Go back and you will see. I will come to you later."

No sooner had she said this than she nimbly turned round and lightly hurried away along the passage. She had her hair done up in the "butterfly" style. I could espy her fair neck under the black hair. Quite striking was her black satin obi, wound round her shapely waist. Perhaps the satin lined only one side of the sash, I reflected as I stood watching her.

IV

With absolutely no thought of any kind in my head, I returned to my room, and found it dusted clean and tidied up carefully. Then I recalled last night's apparition, and felt an irresistible curiosity to look into the closet. I went up to it and opened the paper screen. I found inside an undersized chest of drawers, with a woman's obi draping down its side, suggesting that somebody had carried away in haste some clothes on the cabinet. One end of the obi was in a layer of folded kimono of feminine colour. Some books on shelves occupied one corner of the closet, one of the Zen[31] priest Haku-un's works, and the classical *Isemono-gatari*, standing out conspicuously among them.

Giving myself no reason, I resumed my seat on the cushion at the low teak wood table, which served as my desk. On the table was my sketch book, carefully placed in the centre, with a pencil between its leaves. I took up the book, wondering how the things I wrote in dreams would look in the morning.

"Kaidono tsuyuo furu-u-ya monogurui."

Somebody wrote this under it: "*Kaidono tsuyuo furu-u-ya asa-garasu.*"[32] Scribbled in pencil, the style of writing was not as clear as it might be; I thought it too stiff for a woman's hand but too flaccid for a man's. Anyway, it was another surprise to me. I went on reading the next piece:

"*Hanano kage onnano kageno oborokana.*"[33]

This had under it: "*Hanano kage, onnano kageo kasanekeri.*"[34] The third piece:

"*Shoichi-i onnami bakete oborozuki,*" was revised beneath into: "*On-zoshi onnani bakete oborozuki.*"[35] Were they meant to be imitations, or corrections, or a vindication? Was the party a fool, or was it an attempt to fool? I gave a puzzling shake to my head.

"Later," she said, I told myself. She might put in her appearance, when the meal was brought in, and I might get some light, then. What time could it be? I looked at my watch, and it was past eleven o'clock. Such a long sleep I had, I thought. To do with only two meals would at this rate be good for my stomach!

I pushed open a paper screen on the right side of my room, and looked out for a sign of last night's fantasy. What I took for an aronia was indeed a tree of that name in blossom; but the garden was smaller than I fancied. The whole place was grown over with dark-green moss, apparently so nice to walk on, and almost burying five or six stepping stones. On the left a red-barked pine tree, growing out from between rocks, some way up the slope of a mountain, stood slantingly overhanging. A little behind the aronia was a thicket

49

and still further beyond, a grove of tall bamboos, scraping the sunny Spring sky. View to the right was shut out by a ridge of roof; but judging from topography, I should say the ground descended in a slow gradient towards the bathhouse.

The mountain had at its foot a hillock and the hillock was surrounded by a belt of level land, about half a mile wide. This belt glided on the outer side into the bottom of the sea, and rose sharply again forty miles away, forming the islet Maya of thirteen miles in circumference. This was the geography of Nakoi. The spa-hotel is built at the foot of the hill, with its back terraced as closely as possible against its steep side, taking in half of its craggy slope for the scenic effect of its garden. The building is two-storeyed in front; but only one at the rear, and sitting at the edge of my verandah, the heels touched the velvety moss. It was no wonder, I had thought last night, that the house was a strangely planned one, with so many steps to go up and down, and up and down.

I now opened the window in the left flank. A natural hollow, a couple of yards, both ways, in a big rock, had turned into a pool of water, one does not know how long since, and was reflecting calmly in it a wild cherry tree in bloom, while a bunch or two of giant-leaved creeping bamboos decked a corner of the rock. Yonder a hedge of what looked like boxthorns fenced in the garden. A road from the beach sloping upward, for climbing the hill, seemed to pass outside the hedge, and passers talking could be heard now again. Off the other edge of the road, orange trees covered the ground that fell Southward, the declivity ending in a great bamboo jungle, that flared white. I learned for the first time, then, that the bamboo leaves shine like silver, when looked at from a distance. Above the jungle, the hill on the other side abounded in pine trees, and five or six stone steps were clearly visible between their red trunks. Probably a temple stood on the hill.

I went out into the verandah and found that it turned square with its railing. An upstairs room across an inner court in the front section of the building filled up space, which should, as I judged from its bearings, give a view of the sea. It was jolly that leaning against the railing, I was upstairs as high. The bath tank being situated in the basement, and from the standpoint of taking a bath I might be said to be living on the third floor.

The house is quite large; but the living quarters and kitchen apart, shutters were down in nearly all the rooms, except the upstairs one in the front section, another next to mine by turning to the right along the verandah, and my own, of course. Evidently I was the only guest stopping there. The rain-doors were all closed; but judging from the look of things I might wager pretty safely that once they opened those doors they would not go to the trouble of shutting them again, even at night. One might even suspect they did not bother themselves about locking the entrance door. I should say, an ideal place for an unhuman sojourn.

It was almost noon by my watch, and I was beginning to feel somewhat empty. But there was no sign of any tiffn forthcoming. Imagining myself a wanderer in the familiar line of poetry, "Void the mountain, not a soul seen," I thought I might do without a meal or so cheerfully. I felt too lazy to paint. As for the poetry, I have been living it, and it appeared to me decidedly unwise to try to compose one. I have brought with me a few books tied into my tripod; but even that I felt in no mood to untie and read. Lying with the shadow of flowers on the verandah, with my back basking in warm sunshine of Spring, I was in the height of worldly delectation. I shall fall off if I thought and a motion was dangerous. If I could help it, I did not want even to breathe, I felt like remaining immobile for a fortnight or so, like a plant growing out of the floor matting.

Presently I heard somebody walking along the passage, and then coming upstairs. As the footsteps neared, I judged there were two. No sooner had they stopped outside my room than one of them went back the way he or she came, without a word. The *karakami* opened and I expected to greet her of this morning. I felt as if I had missed something, when I saw that it was only the young maid of last night.

"Sorry, *Danna-sama*, we kept you waiting." So saying the girl placed a portable dinner table before me, with not a word of reference to the missing breakfast. On the table was a dish of broiled fish with something green, and a lacquered bowl, which, on taking off the cover, revealed a clear soup with some young ferns and some red and white shrimps. The colours of shrimps, were so lovely that I kept looking at them a while.

"You don't like that, *Danna-sama*," asks the girl.

"Yes, I am going to take it," I said; but in my mind I was loath to eat so charming a thing. I remembered reading in a book, that taking some salad into his dish, and looking at, Turner said to one sitting next to him at dinner, that its colour was refreshing and was the one he used. I wished very much that I could have let Turner see the shrimps and the ferns. In my opinion, there is nothing beautiful in colour in Western dishes, excepting perhaps salad and radishes. I cannot, of course, say anything from the nutritious point of view, but I must say that theirs is very uncivilized from the artist's point of view. On the contrary the Japanese dishes are all superbly beautiful, be it the soup, the pastry or the sliced raw fish. You may come away without taking a single chopstickful of things set before you, but you may consider yourself fully repaid for having been at a teahouse, from the point of view of having feasted your eyes.

"There is a young lady, here?" I asked the girl, as I put down the soup bowl.

"Yes, sir."

"Who is she?"

"She is the young Mistress."

"Is there any elder Mistress besides her?"

"She died last year."

"And the master?"

"He lives here, and the lady is his daughter."

"That young lady?"

"Yes, sir."

"Are there any other guests?"

"No, sir."

"Only myself, then?"

"Yes, sir."

"What does the young Mistress do every day?"

"Sewing...."

"And?"

"She plays samisen."[36]

How unexpected! However quite interesting and so:

"What else?" I asked.

"She goes to the temple," answers the girl.

Unexpected again. The samisen playing and the temple going are decidedly a curious conglomeration.

"Does she go there to worship?"

"She goes there to see the *Osho-sama*."[37.]

"Does the *Osho-san* take lessons in samisen?"

"No, sir."

"What does she go there for?"

"She goes there to see Daitetsu-sama."

It dawned on me that Daitetsu must be the priest who wrote the framed calligraphy on the wall. Judging from its wording Daitetsu must be a Zen priest, and Haku-un's book in the closet must belong to him.

"Is this a living room for anyone of the family?"

"Yes, sir; the Mistress lives here."

"Is that so? Well, then, she had been here till I came in, last night?"

"Yes."

"I am sorry, I have robbed her of her room. And what does she go to see Daitetsu-san for?"

"I don't know."

"Anything else?"

"Many other things."

"What many other things?"

"I don't know."

This put an end to my catechism, and also to my tiffn. The girl took away the little table. As she pulled open the wallpapered screen, I saw through the opening the young woman of butterfly coiffeur, resting her chin in her hands that were supported by arms which had their elbows on the railing of the upstairs verandah, overlooking a inner court shrubbery. The "butterfly" was gazing downward with the pose of a modernised goddess of mercy. In contrast to how she struck me this morning, she was serenely calm. Looking downward as she was, I could not tell how her eyes were moving. I could only wonder if any change had come into her expression. An ancient says that nothing speaks better for a person than his pupils. He is right. How can a man conceal? There is, indeed, no organ in human body so alive as the eye. Two real butterflies flew upward twirling around each other from under the railing, on which the human butterfly was leaning quietly. It was just at this juncture that the girl opened the fusuma[38] of my room, and the noise made the woman yonder lift her eyes from the butterflies, and direct them toward me. Her eyes shot through the space like a shaft of rays, and hit me between my own. My heart throbbed; but the same moment the girl closed the screen. The momentary spell broke and I returned to the noon tide of balmy Spring.

I again stretched myself full length on the matted floor, and soon I was reciting:

> "Sadder than the moon's lost light,
>   Lost is the kindling of dawn,
>   To travellers journeying on,
> The shutting of thy fair face from my sight."

Supposing I was in love with the "butterfly" and felt deeply the flash of joy or the pang of a sudden parting like the one I just had, at the very moment when I was

dying to meet her, I should have unquestionably poetised
in a strain something like the above. Furthermore, I may
have added,

> "Might I look on thee in death,
> With bliss I would yield my breath."

these two lines. Fortunately, I had long since left behind
me the common glamour of love and amour, and could
not feel pangs of this kind, even if I would. Nevertheless,
the poetical significance of the event that had just
happened was well brought out in the six lines. Not that
there was any such heart's anguish between the
"butterfly" and myself. I felt it highly entertaining to
think of our present relations in the light of these verses.
Nor was it unpleasant to interpret the meaning of these
lines as reflecting our present condition. There was,
indeed, an invisibly thin line of cause and effect, binding
us together, making real, at least, part of the conditions
sung in these lines. The thread of cause and effect
occasions no worry when as thin as this. Besides, it is no
ordinary thread, but is like the rainbow spanning the
sky; like the haze screening horizon; and like the
spiderweb sparkling with dew. It may break at any
moment if wanted to be broken; but it is exquisitely
beautiful while it remains and is seen. But what if the
thread should, all of a sudden, grow thick and stout as a
halyard? No fear: I am an artist and she is not of a
common kind.

Suddenly the fusuma opened again, and I rolled my
body round to look that way. There was standing in the
opening, the "butterfly," the other end of cause and

effect, holding up in her hand a celadon porcelain bowl on a tray.

"Lying down again? It must have been annoying to you to be disturbed so often, last night, ho, ho, ho," she laughed. She betrayed not the least sign of having been impressed with fear or of fearing, still less with a bashful feeling. The only thing was, she got the start of me.

"Thank you, this morning," I said my thanks again. This was the third time I made acknowledgment for the deshabille, and each time it consisted of the two words "Thank you."

I made a move to sit up; but she was quicker; she had sat down on the matting close to where I was lying:

"Oh, please don't stir. You can talk as you are, Sensei."[39.]

I thought her quite convincing and only changed my pose so far as to lie on my belly, with my chin on the ends of two arms, planted in on the tatami-mat.

"I have come to make tea for you, Sensei, thinking you must be tired of doing nothing."

"Thank you." I said it again. I saw, in the sea-green cake-bowl she brought, some isinglass paste *yokan*. I love *yokan*. Not that I am eager to eat it, but to me it appeals decidedly as an objet d'art, with its fine, smooth surface, that glistens semi-transparently as the light strikes it. Especially pleasant-looking is the one of light-green, with its lustre and its appearance of being wrought with marble and *gyoku*-stone. In a celadon bowl, it looks as if just born out of it. It makes me feel like putting out my hand and feeling it. No Western cake, that I know of, produces such delicious impression as the *yokan*. Cream is agreeably soft in colour, but there is something heavy and thick about it, while jelly with all its look of a precious stone, trembles so that it is devoid of the weightiness of the *yokan*. It is an insuperable abomination when it comes to a tower of flour, milk and sugar.

"Oh, very nice."

"Gembey has just brought it back from the town. I hope it is good enough for your taste."

Gembey must have stopped overnight in the town, I thought; but I made no answer. It made no difference to me where the thing was got or by whom. The thing being beautiful, I should be content with thinking that it is beautiful.

"This celadon bowl is exquisite in shape and superb in tint. It makes a worthy match to the *yokan*."

The woman smiled a smile that betrayed a shadow of contempt playing about her mouth. It was probable that she thought I was jesting. If that is the case, my words, I must confess, fully deserved contumely. When a witless fellow tries to be jocular, he generally lands himself on a sorry exhibition of this kind.

"Is this Chinese?"

"I have no idea." The celadon had no place in her eyes.

"Somehow it appears Chinese to me." I looked at its base by holding up the bowl.

"Do you take interest in things of that sort, Sensei? Would you like to see more?"

"Yes, indeed."

"Father is very fond of bric-a-brac and has quite a collection. I shall tell father about you, and let him invite you to a cup of tea."

Tea? The word called up before me a picture I am not very enthusiastic about. In fact it made me shrink back. I am persuaded that there is no refined idler that so unwarrantably puts on airs as the frothing tea imbiber. He almost suffocatingly narrows the wide world of poetry and does things most self-importantly, most over-studiedly and most hair-splittingly. He drinks of foamy froth in altogether unnecessarily abject humility, and finds himself in the seventh heaven of joy. Such is the tea man. If there be any pleasure and interest in this intricate tangle of rules, then the denizens of the regimental barracks at Azabu must have joys and pleasures knocking about their nose. The "right-turn!" and "march-on!" lads must be all great tea men. Pshaw! They—the so-called tea-men—are, to tell the truth, merchants, tradesmen, and the like; with no real taste-culture, who have no idea of what makes nature-loving refinement, and swallow mechanically the tea-rules adopted since the days of the great tea-master, Rikyu, of three centuries ago, and delude themselves into being men of refinement. Theirs is a trick to make fools of real men of nature-loving refinement.

"Tea? You mean the tea drinking ceremony?"

"No, Sensei; but tea with no ceremony, which you need not drink if you don't wish to, take a cup or even two."

"If that is the kind, then, I may just as well."

"Father is very fond of showing his collection."

"Must I praise them to the skies?"

"Well, Sensei, he is growing old and compliments gladden him."

"I may go about it lightly then."

"You may be generous into the bargain."

"Ha, ha, ha, ha. Pardon my observing that you do not speak the countryside language."

"Not in language, but in person, you mean?"

"In personality it is better for one to be of the countryside."

"Then I may give myself airs?"

"But you have lived in Tokyo?"

"Yes, I have been there, and also in Kyoto. I am a bird of passage and I have been in many places."

"Which do you like best, here or the capital?"

"It is all the same to me."

"You feel more at home in a quiet place like this, don't you?"

"At home, or not at home, the life in this world depends all upon how you train your mind. It would be of no use to move into a land of mosquitoes, when you got sick of the country of fleas."

"It would be all well if you emigrated into a country, where there were neither mosquitoes nor fleas?"

"If there be any such country, just show it to me, please Sensei. Show it to me now," says the woman earnestly.

"If you wish, I certainly will." I took out my sketch book and let my brush spin out a woman on horse back, looking up to a mountain cherry blossom—just an imaginary impression. A work of the instant, it hardly made a picture, but to give an idea. I speedily finished it and said:

"Now get in here, there is neither flea nor mosquito in this land," putting it under her nose. Will she be seized by a surprise or by bashfulness? To judge by her looks, I felt sure that embarrassment would be the last thing she would allow to overtake her. I watched her for the moment.

"What a cramped up world! It is all width. You are fond of a place like this? You must be a regular crab." Thus she got herself out, and I laughed out aloud:

"Ha, ha, ha, ha."

A sweet warbler that had come near the eve of the house, broke its note in the middle of its song and hopped to a tree a little way off. We purposely stopped our talk and listened in silence; but the little throat that lost its tune would not recover it easily.

"You met Gembey on the mountain, yesterday, Sensei?"

"Yes, my lady."

"You made a detour to see the 'five elements' tomb of the Maid of Nagara?"

"Even like the dew drop, that when autumn comes lodges trembling on grass, must I roll off to die." The woman recited the lines, just the words only, with no tune or intonation. I did not know what for, but volunteered the information:

"I heard that song at the tea stall."

"The old woman told you then. Long ago she was with us as our servant here, before I...." Here she looked at me, and I pretended to know nothing.

"It was when I was young. I used to tell her the story of Nagarano Otome, every time she called on us after leaving here. The song was very difficult for her to remember. But hearing if told her so often, she finally got everything by heart."

"That accounts for it; I thought she knew a very literary sort of thing for a woman of her station—however that song is a sad one."

"Sad, do you think? If I were that maiden, I would have never sung like that. In the first place, what good will it serve to throw yourself into a river and die?"

"None whatever. What would you have done?"

"What would I have done? Why it is easy enough. I would have made sweethearts of both Sasada Otoko and Sasabe Otoko."

"Both?"

"Yes, yes."

"You are great."

"Not great at all; but only natural."

"Now I see, you can thus get along without flying into the land of fleas or the land of mosquitoes?"

"You see, you can live on without feeling like a crab?"

"*Hoh ho-ke-kyo*," the warbler recovered its note, which it had almost lost, and vindicated the fact with loudness that was wholly unexpected. Once recovered, the song seemed to flow out of its own accord, as the bird held down its head, quivered its swelling throat, opened its mouth as wide as it could, and kept on:

"*Hoh ho-ke-kyo. Hoh hokke-kyo....*"

The bird went on without stopping, and the woman took the trouble to tell me:

"That is the real poetry."

V

"Pardon, *Danna*[40] but may I ask you if you are from Tokyo?"

"Do I look from Tokyo?"

"Look? Why a glance... your language tells."

"Can you tell where in Tokyo?"

"Well, that is a puzzler; Tokyo is so large.... Let me see. You cannot be from downtown. You must belong to uptown. The uptown parts are... Kojimachi, eh? Or Koishikawa? If not, you must be from Ushigome or Yotsuya?"

"Somewhere around there. You seem to know Tokyo well?"

"Well, I am Tokyo-born, *Danna*, look what I may."

"No wonder, I thought you looked a city man."

"Aha, he, he, he, it is all up with a fellow, *Danna*, when he comes down to this."

"What made you to drift into a place like this?"

"You are right, *Danna*, it is drifted that I have done. I had gone down so low that I could not go lower, and had to say goodbye to Tokyo."

"You ran a barbershop from the beginning?"

"No, not ran, *Danna*, I am only a journeyman barber. There is a block named Matsunagacho, a dingy small place... a gentleman like you don't know it, of course. But Ryukan-bashi... you don't know that either, eh? It is a pretty well known bridge...."

"I say, give me little more soap, won't you? It hurts."

"It hurts? I am very particular about shaving, *Danna*. I never consider my work done, until I have gone over along and then gone over contrariwise, cutting each individual hair at the very root. No, what the latter-day barbers do is not shaving but letting the razor slide over the face. Bear it a bit more and you will be done."

"Bear I have done, quite a while now. There is a good fellow, put some warm water, if not soap."

"You can stand no longer? My shaving never hurts. The fact is, you have allowed your beard to grow too long without shaving."

The barber reluctantly let go my cheek, which he was pinching with the force of clinched nippers, and taking down a thin apology of a red cake of soap, he had no sooner wetted it in a basin of water than he went all over my face with it. To have a piece of soap applied directly to the skin of my face was one of my rarest experiences in barber shops, and I was not over-pleased to see that the water in which the soap was dipped had the appearance of having stood there for some days!

Sitting in a barber's chair, I was called upon, in vindication of my right as a customer, to look into a mirror. I have been thinking, for sometime, however, if I should not waive this right. A mirror owes it to itself that its surface is perfectly even and flat, and the image it reflects shall be faithful to the original. If the owner of a mirror, which is not possessed of this common quality, forces you to look into it, you may charge him, as you will a poor photographer, with intentionally injuring your looks. Snubbing the vain may serve cultural purposes; but I fail to see the justice of insulting you by calling a reflection your face, which makes a mockery of it. The mirror, which I was expected to exercise patience to look into, has decidedly been insulting me. I slightly turn my face right, and the mirror makes all nose of it. I turn left, and my mouth extends clear up to the ears. I look a perfect picture of a crushed toad, when I turn my eyes upward. My head elongates itself limitlessly, the moment I incline it ever so little forward. I must make of myself monsters of all imaginable variety as long as I sit before this mirror. Who can say that I was not undergoing a torture?

Moreover, this barber was no common barber. He appeared human enough, when I first looked in, and saw him depositing tobacco ashes from his long pipe on a toy flag of Anglo-Japanese Alliance, apparently feeling very wearisome. But fear crept into me, the moment I walked in and gave him the custody of my head; for a doubt arose in me whether the right of ownership of my cranium and parts appertaining passed completely to him or whether I still retained a small fraction of it myself. His handling of my head! I felt that it could not remain there much longer, even if it were nailed onto my shoulders.

His manner of using the razor showed him to be a perfect stranger to the rules of civilization. The weapon made a most bloodcurdling sound, when scraping across my cheek. As it came to the tuft of hair by the ear, the artery almost snapped. About the chin, it sported itself making a noise as of somebody crunching the frost raised ground. The most dreadful part of the story was that this barber considered himself the most skilful tonsor in the land.

Lastly, the man was well loaded with something of fairly strong flavour. Every time he said *Danna*, a smell accompanied the word and a gust of highly-charged gas attacked my nose. At this rate there was no telling when or where his razor might make a jaunt of its own. The man using it having no definite plan to guide him, it was impossible that I, who placed my head in his custody, should have any idea of it. I should not grumble as my head was in his hands as part of a legitimate understanding. But what, if he should change his mind and set about cutting my throat?

"It is only fellows who are not sure of their hand that use soap. But it cannot be helped, perhaps, in your case, because you are too hairy, *Danna*." So protesting my man put the soap back to the shelf; but disobeying his wish, it fell to the clay floor.

"I don't think I have seen much of you around here, *Danna*. You have come here lately?"

"Why, yes, I came here, only a few days ago."

"Is that so? Where are you stopping?"

"At Shiota Hotel."

"You are a guest at Shiota, are you? That was what I thought. To tell you the truth I came here looking for help from the old gentleman of Shiota. I used to know him, located near him as I was, while he lived in Tokyo. He is a fine old man, knowing what is what. He lost his wife last year, and he now passes most of his time in toying with his curios and things. He is said to have great things, which would bring in a good little fortune if sold."

"Has he not got a pretty daughter?"

"Look out, there!"

"What for?"

"Why? You may not know it, but she is a divorcee."

"So, eh?"

"You don't seem to make much of it, *Danna*; but it was an affair. It was not at all necessary that she should take a divorce.... The bank busted and she left her husband, because she could no longer go in for a high living. She may be all right, as long as the old man is there; but if anything should happen to him, she would be lost in the sea."

"You think so?"

"Of course I do, and she and her elder brother, who is now the head of the family are no friends at all."

"The head of the family?"

"Yes, the old man is retired, and family affairs are in the charge of his son, who lives upon the hill. It is a fine place he lives in, with a most beautiful view. You should have a look at it."

"Oh, say give me another coat of soap. It is hurting again."

"Your skin must be very soft. It is because your beard is too tough. You must have a shave at least once in three days. If my shave hurts you, you can't stand it anywhere else."

"I shall do so in future. Or I may have it every day."

"You are going to stay so long? Do you know that you are running a risk? I should say, don't. No good will come out of it. You don't know what trouble you will bring upon yourself by getting tangled up in a silly affair."

"Why?"

"Ah, *Danna*, that woman is pretty to look at; but you must know that she is not right in the head."

"Why?"

"Why? The villagers all say she is crazy."

"There must be some mistake about that."

"No, we have a proof that it is not. Don't, *Danna*, it is risky."

"I am perfectly safe. What kind of proof do you have?"

"Well, it is a queer affair. Light a cigarette and take your time, and I shall tell.... Will you have a shampoo?"

"No thanks."

"Let me then shake off the dandruff a little."

The barber put his ten fingers, which ended in well grown nails, loaded with goodly deposits of dirt, upon my cranium, and set them in motion most violently, forward and backward. The formidable nails ploughed the root of each hair in my head like a rake in the hand of a giant combing a field of wild grass with the power and swiftness of a hurricane. I do not know how many hundreds of thousands of hair there are in my head; I only felt that every one of my capillary growth was being uprooted, leaving the skin in wales, in addition to making the skull and the grey matter of brains vibrate most violently. So strongly did the man rummage my head.

"How do you feel, now? Wasn't that good?"

"You went at it pretty lively."

"Eh? Everybody feels clear in head after my scrub."

"I feel as if my head is dropping away."

"You are feeling so tired? It is the weather does it. Spring makes you feel lazy. Have a smoke. You must feel lonesome, *Danna*, stopping alone at Shiota? You must drop in to see me. The Tokyo-born likes the Tokyo-born. Your talk won't fall in with others. Does the *O-Jo-san* come out to say nice things to you? The trouble with her is she is all mixed up about right and wrong."

"You were going to say something about *O-Jo-san*, and then you went about scrubbing my head and I felt as it was coming off."

"That was so. My head is so empty and I skip about so. I was going to say that the priest fell head over ears in love with her."

"The priest? What priest?"

"The priestling of Kaikanji, of course."

"You haven't said a word about a priest, full-fledged or half fledged."

"Haven't I? I am so hasty, *Danna*. The priest, that priestling, was good in looks, of a cast that girls like. This *bozu*[41] became, I tell you, smitten by her of Shiota and at last wrote her a love letter.... Wait a bit, did he go at it himself? No, it was, he wrote.... Let me see.... I am getting mixed up.... No, I am all right, I've got it... so was in fright and consternation."

"Who was in fright and consternation?"

"The woman, of course."

"By receiving the letter?"

"That would be a saving grace if she were. But she is not of the kind to get scared."

"Who was it really, then, that was in fright and consternation?"

"Why, he that spoke to her of his love."

"I thought he did not go at it personally."

"Oh, chuck it. It is all wrong. By receiving the letter, can't you see?"

"Why then it must be the woman, who was in fright and consternation."

"No, the man."

"If man, then it must be the priest?"

"Yes, the priest, of course."

"But what scared him so?"

"What scared him? Why, he, the priest, was in the temple assisting the abbot in the afternoon service. Then all of a sudden, the woman rushed into the temple.... Lord, she must be off a great deal."

"Did she do anything?"

"'If I am so dear to you, come let us make love before our all mighty Buddha,' she said and hugged him by the neck!"

"Ho?"

"Consternation was no word, for poor Taian, the priest. He got all the shame he wanted by writing to a lunatic, and, disappearing that night, he died."

"Died?"

"At least I think he must have killed himself. He could not have outlived the shame."

"I don't know about that."

"Maybe he is still living somewhere. Death would not have come out so well, the other party being a mad woman."

"Very interesting, indeed."

"Interesting is no word for it. Why the affair set the whole village a-roaring with laughter. But the woman, being off her mind, was all indifference as she still is. All will be well for a man so sober like you, *Danna*; but the party being what she is, you don't know what mess you will get into, if you try to flirt with her."

"I have got to be careful, eh? Ha, ha, ha!"

The Spring breeze came lazily wafting from the genially warm beach, and set the entrance curtain of the barber's shop flapping sleepily, and a swallow cast its flitting shadow in the mirror before me, as it dived under the curtain with its body half turned. Under the eve of a house on the other side of the road, a sexagenarian sat squatting on a slightly raised seat, and was busy shelling bivalves in silence. Every time a small knife went in between shells, a small flabby lump fell into a basket, and the empty shells were thrown away, two feet across the gossamer, there adding to the height of a sparkling heap. Now and again the heap collapsed, sending the oyster, clam, and other shells down into a small brook, to be buried forever in its sandy bed. In no time the heap grew again under a willow tree; but the old man was too busy to think of a life beyond molluscs; he only went on throwing meatless shells upon gossamer. His basket seemed to be bottomless and his Spring day endless.

The sandy stream ran under a twelve yard bridge, carrying the warm water of Spring toward the sea shore. Down where Spring's water joined the tide of the sea, numberless fishing nets were drying in the sun, hanging from erect poles of longer or shorter lengths and were giving, one might suspect, a fish-smelling warmth to the soft breeze wafting towards the village through their meshes. And one saw between them the placid face of the sea, undulating slowly like molten lead.

No harmony was possible between this scenery and my barber. If he were a man of strong personality, strong enough to impress me as powerfully as the scenery around, I should have been struck with a sense of great incongruity. Fortunately, however, my man was not so striking a character. However Tokyo-born, however high-spiritedly he might talk, he was no match for the all genial and all embracing influence of nature. My barber has been essaying to break up this all subjugating power of nature with all his caustic effervescences; but instead he has been swallowed up and was floating in the light wave of Spring, not leaving a trace of the loud-talking Tokyo-born barber. Inconsistency is a phenomenon to be found between persons or things of equal standing, but possessed of hopeless incompatibility in strength, spirit or physique. When distance is very great between the two, inconsistency wears out, and will, instead, assume activity only as part of a superior power. Thus it happens that cleverness becomes a willing servant of greatness; the unintelligent of the clever; and horses and cattle of the unintelligent. My barber is making a comic exhibition of himself, with the beautiful scenery of Spring for his background. He who tries to spoil the calm Springy feeling is only adding to the profundity of that feeling. This man of very cheap vaporing cannot but prove after all a colour in full harmony with the Spring afternoon, which is symbolic of gloriousness.

My man would make rather a good picture, and poetry, too, when studied in this light, and I stayed talking with him long after my shave was over, when a small head of a young priest put in an appearance, slipping in by the entrance curtain and said:

"A shave please."[42]

The newcomer was a jolly-looking little priest in an old-fashioned grey cotton clothes, held together by a coil of light but cotton-wadded belt, under a mosquito-net-like cloak.

"You got a scolding, didn't you, the other day, for loafing, Ryonen-san?"

"No, I was complimented."

"Complimented for catching minnows on your way to an errand, were you?"

"The *Osho-san* praised me, saying: 'You did well Ryonen, to take your time in play, young though you are.'"

"That accounts, eh? You have got many swellings in your head. Too much trouble to shave a bumpy head like this; but I let you off this time. Don't come again with a freak of a head like this."

"Thanks, I shall go to a better barber when my head is in good shape."

"Ha, ha, ha, this zigzag thing has got a tongue to talk with to be sure."

"Poor in work, but quite up in boozing, that is what you are, arn't you?"

"Poor in work? Say it again...."

"Not I, but it is the *Osho-san* who says it. Don't get so mad, if you know how old you are."

"Humph, the idea! Isn't that so *Danna*?"

"Ya—eh?"

"Priests, they live high above the stone steps, and have nothing much to look after. That must be what makes them so free in tongue. Even this little fellow can talk so. There lay down your head—lay down, I say, do you hear? I will cut you if you don't do as I tell you. You understand? The red thing will run."

"It hurts! Don't be so rough."

"If you can't stand this sort of thing, how can you expect to be a priest?"

"I am one already."

"But not full feathered yet. Oh, say, by the way, how did Taian-san die?"

"Taian-san is not dead."

"Not dead? He must be dead."

"Taian-san has got a new spirit and is now hard at his study at Taibaiji temple in Rikuzen. Everybody expects he will make a great priest by and by. A very good thing, indeed."

"What is good? Priests may have their way; but it cannot be good even for them to decamp at night? You ought to be careful, you young one, it is woman who brings you trouble. Speaking of a woman, does that crazy thing still come to the *Osho-san*?"

"I have never heard of a woman named 'Crazy Thing.'"

"You blockhead, tell me, does she come or does she not."

"No crazy woman comes; but Mr. Shiota's daughter comes."

"The *Osho-san* may be great; but he won't be able to make anything of the poor girl. She is possessed by her former husband."

"That lady is a very worthy woman. The *Osho-san* speaks highly of her."

"That beats all. Everything is topsy-turvy up there, above the stone steps. Whatever the *Osho-san* may say, the mad must be mad—Here now, all shaved. Hurry home and get another scolding."

"No, not yet. I shall take little more time to get a good opinion of the *Osho-san*."

"Do as you please, you long-tongued brat."

"Go on, you dry rot."

"What!"

But the clean shaved head dived under and was on the other side of the curtain, the Spring breeze softly fanning it.

VI

I sat at my desk, as the sun was going down. I had opened wide all the paper screens and doors of my room. The people of the hotel are not many, but its building is extensive. My room is far in the interior, with many turns of passage, separating it from the quarters inhabited by the not many people of the establishment, and no sound comes to disturb my thinking. It has been especially quiet today. I even fancied that the proprietor, his daughter, the young maid and the man servant had all gone away unknown to me. Had they done so, they could not, I thought, have gone to an ordinary place; they must have flown to a land of hazes, or of cloud—so far, far away that it may be reached only after floating lazily on the sea, carelessly and too lazy to steer, until drifted to where the white sail became indistinguishable from cloud or water, and indeed the sail itself could not tell whether it was the cloud or water. Otherwise they must have vanished, swallowed up in the spirit of Spring, the elements of which they are composed returning to an invisible ether, untraceable in the great expanse of space even with the help of a microscope.

They might have become the lark and flown to where the evening dusk was deepening into purple, after they have sung out the golden yellow of the rape flowers. Or else they might be sweetly sleeping out the world a captive under a fallen camellia flower, failing to steal its nectar, after having served to draw out lengthily the long Spring day, by turning into a gadfly. So quiet was the day.

The Spring breeze passed freely through the empty house not necessarily as a duty to those who welcomed it, nor yet out of spite to those who resented it. It came naturally and went naturally, a reflection of the impartial universe. With my chin resting in the palms of my hands, my mind was as free and open as my room, and the breeze would, uninvited, pass in and out with perfect freedom.

You think of treading on, and you fear the earth might crack open under you. You know the sky is hanging over you, and you dread lightning might flash out and smite you. You are urged that you fail your manhood unless you assert your antagonism and the world becomes a place of endless trouble. To him that lives under the firmament that has its East and West and has to walk on the rope of interests, true love is one's enemy and visible wealth dirt. A name made and honour won may be likened unto honey which wise bees leave behind by forgoing their sting, after making it appear that they were manufacturing and sweetening it. The so-called pleasures all come from love for things and contain in them all kinds of pain. However, the world happens to have its poet and artist, who feed on the essence of this world of relativity, and knows the absolute principle of purity. They dine on heaven's haze and quench their thirst with dew. They talk of purple and discuss crimson, and no regret detains them when death comes for them. Their pleasures are not to become attached to things, but to become themselves part of things. When they have become things themselves, they find no room for their ego though they may explore the remotest confines of the earth. They rise above worldly dirt and drink full of the boundless air of purity. These things are said not merely to scare those saturated with the odor of the lucre of the city, and alone to pose loftily, but to convey the gospel contained in them and to invite their brother beings to share in its blessings. To tell the truth, art and poetry are principles all men are born with. Most people, who, having counted their summers, are now living their grey winter, will be able to reawaken their past with its joys of seeing light shining in them. He who is unable to recall such a memory is one who has lived a life not worth living.

I do not say that the poet's joys consist in giving oneself exclusively over to one thing, or surrendering ourselves solely to another. He may, at one time enter and become a solitary flower, or turn into a butterfly at another. Or like Wordsworth become a field of daffodils, with his heart thrown into confusion by the wind. Sometimes again he becomes lost in a scene and is unable clearly to tell what is it that has captured his heart. Some people may call this being possessed by nature. Others may describe it as the heart listening to a music of an unstrung harp. Still others may see in it a lingering in boundless regions or wandering in a limitless expanse, being unable to know or to understand. Say what they like, they are perfectly free to do so. I was precisely in this state of mind as I sat resting half of my weight on my bent elbow that rested on my desk, with my head perfectly vacant otherwise.

It was unmistakably clear that I was thinking nothing, looking at nothing. I could not be said to have become or turned into anything, as there was nothing of striking colours moving within my world of consciousness. Nevertheless I was in motion. I might not be moving in the world; but I was anyhow in motion. Not moved by a flower, not moved by birds, not moved against humanity, still moving as in a spell.

If I must explain this state of being somehow less oracularly, I should say that my soul was moving with the Spring. I should say that an etherial essence, obtained by compounding all the colours, forces, substances and sounds of Spring into an esoteric electuary, then by melting it in dews gathered in the land of immortals, and by finally evaporating it in the sunshine of fairyland, found its way into my pores before I became aware, and put me into my present state. Ordinarily an absorption is accompanied by a stimulus, which will make the process pleasant. In my case, how I came to it was quite hazy no stimulation accompanying it. Because of this absence of stimulation, there was something indescribably profound in my joy, which was quite different from those that are transparent and noisy, and occasion superficial excitement. Mine might be likened unto a great expanse of ocean, moving from its unseen fathomless depth from continent to continent, except that there was not quite as much active vitality. But I was the more fortunate because of this deficiency, as the manifestation of great vitality must needs anticipate its exhaustion some day. There is no such worry in the normality of things. My mind was presently in a state more airy than normal and I was not only free from all anxiety that strong activity might wear out, but I was above the common level of indifferent normality. By airiness I mean simply elusiveness, and do not imply any idea of over-weakness. Poets speak of melting airiness or downy lightness, and the phrase exactly fits the condition I am describing.

I wondered next, how it would work to make a picture of my fancy. I doubted not for a moment that it would not make an ordinary picture. An everyday painting is a mere reproduction, on a piece of silk or canvas of what one sees around, as it is, or else after filtering it through an aesthetic eye. A picture has done its part, when a flower looks the flower it is, the water as it reflects in the eye, and human characters animate as in life. If one is to rise above this common level, one must let live on the canvas one's theme, with touches that utter sentiments exactly as one feels about it. Since the artists of this order aim at working the special impressions they have received into the phenomena they have caught, they may not be said to have produced a picture, unless their brush speaks, at its every sweep, of those impressions. Their work must bear out their claim that their manner of perceiving this way and feeling that way has in no way been influenced by or borrowed from old traditions or those going before them, but that nevertheless theirs is the most correct and beautiful. Otherwise they are not entitled to call the work their own.

Workers of the two classes are one in waiting for definite outside impulses before they take up their brush, whatever differences there may be in their depth and in the manner they treat their subjects. But in my case, the subject I wished to treat was not so clearly defined. I roused my senses to the highest pitch of wakefulness; but I looked in vain for a shape, colour, shade, and lines thick and thin, in the objects without me, to suit my fancy. My feelings had not come from without; but even if they had, I could not raise my finger and point at their cause as such distinctly, as they formed no definite object of perception. All that there were, were only feelings, and the question was how those feelings might be depicted to make a picture, nay how I might give them expression so that others might, by looking at my production, feel as I was feeling as nearly as possible.

An ordinary picture requires no feeling, but only the object to reproduce. A picture of a higher order necessitates there existing the object and feeling; one of the class still higher has nothing for its life but feelings, and an object that will fit in with such feelings must be caught to make a picture. But such an object is not easily forthcoming, and even if it came, it would be no easy work to arrange it appropriately. Even if arranged successfully, its presentation would take such a form as would sometimes make it appear totally different from anything in nature, so much so that it would make no picture at all for ordinary people. The artist himself would not recognise that his production represented anything in existence, but that his was only an attempt to convey, however fractionally, his feelings at the very moment when his fancy was aroused. He would consider it a most creditable achievement if he, after scouring the length and breadth of the country, with not a moment of forgetfulness, comes suddenly, at the cross roads upon his lost child and folds it in his arms, not giving time even for lightning to flash, saying, "Why you were here, my child." But that is where the rub comes in. If I can only work out this tone, I shall not care what others may say of my picture. I shall, with the least concern, let them say it is not a picture at all. If my combination of colours, gave expression to my feelings even in part; if the straight and curve of the lines spoke for a fraction of this spirit; if the general disposition of the picture conveyed any of the superprosaic thoughts, I shall not mind if the thing to assume a shape in the picture should happen to be a horse, or a cow or something neither a horse nor a cow. No, I shall not mind; but the trouble was nothing would come forth to fit my fancy. I laid my sketch book open on my desk and looked down upon it until my eyes almost fell through it. It was useless.

I laid my pencil aside and thought; thought it was a mistake, to begin with, that I should have tried to make a picture of abstract feelings. Men are not so different from one another and there must have been some who have had the same touch of thought as I have and must have tried to perpetuate such feelings by some means or other. By what means I wondered.

Music! The word flashed across my mind. Yes, music must be the voice of nature, born under such necessity, under such circumstances. It occurred, for the first time, to me, then, that music is something that must be listened to and that must be learned. Unfortunately, I am a perfect stranger to music.

I wondered next if my fancy would not make poetry, and ventured to step into the third dominion. In my memory, it was an individual named Lessing, who arguing that the province of poetry are events that occur conditioned on the passing of time, established the fundamental principle that poetry and painting are not one but two different arts. Seen in this light, poetry seems to give little promise of making anything out of the situation of things, to which I have been struggling to give expression. The physical condition of my feeling of joy may have in it the element of time, but does not consist of an event that progressively developed in the flow of time. My joy is joyous not because No. 1 goes away and No. 2 comes in its place, and not because No. 3 is born as No. 2 vanishes. I am joyful because my joy is felt deeply and retained from the beginning. Say this in an everyday language, and there will be no need of making a factor of time. Poetry, like painting, will come of things arranged separately. Only what scene and sentiment to bring into the poetry, to portray this expansive and abandoned condition is the question. Poetry should be forthcoming, in spite of Lessing, so soon as these factors are caught. Homer and Virgil may be let alone. If poetry be fit to give voice to a mood, that mood may be painted in words without being under time restrictions and unaided by an event that progresses in an orderly manner, as long as the simple spatial requirements of painting are fulfilled.

The point of my pencil began to move slowly, very slowly at first, then with more speed on my sketch book and in half an hour I got these lines:

> "Spring two or three months old,
> Sadness is long as sweet young plants.
> Flowers fall on the empty garden,
> In the soulless hall lies a plain harp.
> Immobile the spider in its maze hangs
> Winding travels blue smoke up the bamboo
> beams."

Reading the six lines over, I thought each of them might make a picture and wondered why I had not set about drawing from the first. I discussed with myself why it is easier to poetise than to paint. Having come so far, I felt the rest ought not to be so very difficult to follow, though a desire seized me that I should now sing a sentiment that defied colour and brush. The squeezing my head this way and that way yielded more lines:

> "Not a word uttered sitting alone,
> But a small light I see in the heart.
> Unwontedly troublesome are human affairs.
> Who shall forget this state?
> Enjoying one day's quiet
> I know now how I passed hundreds of busy
> years.
> My yearning, where shall I communicate?
> Far, far away, in the land of white clouds."

I read the whole piece over again. It was not so very poor; but as a depiction of ethereal conditions I had just experienced, I felt something still wanting. I might try to compose one more piece, and with the pencil still between my fingers, I happened to look out of the opened door way of my room to see at beautiful vision flitting across the three feet space. What could it have been?

I now turned my eyes fully toward the doorway and the vision had half disappeared behind the screen that stood pushed to one side. It had apparently been moving before it caught my eyes, and had now gone out of sight altogether as I stared in amazement toward it. I stopped composing poetry, and instead I now kept my eyes fixed on the open space in the doorway.

The clock had not ticked a full second when the vision returned from the opposite direction to that which it had disappeared. It was that of a slim woman in a wedding gown with long sleeves, walking gracefully along the upstairs verandah of the wing of the hotel, flanking my room. I did not know why, but the pencil fell from my fingers, and the breath I was inhaling through my nose stopped of its own accord. The sky was darkening, as if forewarning one of the cherry season showers, to hasten the evening dusk; but the gowned figure kept on appearing and disappearing in the heavily-charged atmosphere, walking with benign gentleness along the verandah, twelve yards away from me, overlooking an inner court.

The woman said nothing, nor looked either way. She was walking so softly that the rustling of her silk gown seemed scarcely to catch her ears. Some figures—I could not tell what from the distance—adorned the skirt of her dress, and the figured and unfigured parts shaded into each other like day into night. And the woman was indeed, walking in the borderland of night and day.

What mystified me was what made her go so persistently to and from along the verandah, dressed in her long-sleeved gown. Nor had I any idea of how long she had been at this strange exercise in her strange attire. There was, of course, no telling of her purpose. This figure of a woman, appearing and disappearing across the open doorway, repeating the incomprehensible movements, could not help arousing a singular feeling in me. Could it be that she was moved by her regret for the departing Spring, or how could she be so absorbed? If so absorbed, why should she be dressed in such finery?

That resplendent obi, that stood out so strikingly in the hue of departing Spring, lingering at the threshold of gathering dusk, could it be gold brocade? I fancied the bright ornament, moving backward and forward, enshrouded in the gray of approaching night, was like glittering stars in the early dawn of a Spring day; that every second went out one by one, in this distant depth and then in that of the vast vault of heavens, vanishing gradually into the deepening purple.

Another fancy struck me as the door of night was gradually opening to swallow into its darkness this flowery vision. Super-nature! this sight of fading away from the world of colours, with not a sign of regret, nor of struggle, instead of shining an object of admiration in the midst of golden screens and silver lights. But there she was with the shadow of darkness closing in on her, pacing up and down rhythmically, the very picture of composure, and betraying no disposition to hurry or dismay, but calmly going over the same ground again and again. If it be that she knew not the blackness falling upon her, she must be a creature of extreme innocence. If she knew but did not mind it as blackness, then, there must be something uncanny about her. Black must be her native home, and thus may she be resignedly surrendering her visionary existence to return to her realm of darkness, walking so leisurely between the seen and unseen worlds. The inevitable blackness into which the figures adorning her long-sleeves shaded seemed to hint where she had come from.

My imagination took another turn, bringing before me a vision of a beautiful person, beautifully sleeping. Sleeping, alive she breathes herself away into death, without ever awakening. This must break the heart of those watching anxiously around the bed. If struggling in pain and agony, the dear ones attending might think it merciful that death came at once, to say nothing of the wish of the patient to whom life had become not worth living. But what fault could the innocent child have been guilty of that she should be snatched away in a peaceful sleep? To be carried away to Hades while in sleep is like being betrayed into a surprise and having life taken before the mind is made up. If death it must be, the dying should be made to resign to Fate, and one should like to say a prayer or two, yielding to the inevitable. But if the fact of death alone was made clear, before its conditions had been fulfilled, and if one had a voice to say a prayer, one would use that same voice in hallooing, to call, even forcibly back, the soul that has put one step in the other world. To one passing away in sleep, it may be hard to have the soul called back, pulled back, as it were, by the bond of worries of life that would otherwise break, and that one may feel like saying:

"Don't call me back; let me sleep." Nevertheless those around would wish to call aloud. I thought I might call that woman in the verandah the next time she came into view, to wake her up from her waking sleep. But my tongue lost its power of speech no sooner had she passed the opening like a dream. Without fail, the next time, I thought. But again she passed and disappeared before I could utter a word. I was asking myself how this could be, when again she passed, and appeared not to care a rap that she was being watched by one who was in a frenzied state of mind about her. She passed and repassed in a manner that told that one like me had never at all entered her mind. As I was repeating my "next time" in my mind, the dark cloud above let down, as if no longer able to hold back, a screen of fine, soft rain, dismally shutting out the shadow of the woman.

VII

Chilly! With a towel in hand I went downstairs for a warm dip. Leaving my clothes in a small chamber, four more steps downward brought me into the bath room which was about eight mats in size. Stones appeared plentiful, in these parts, the floor of the room being paved with fine granite, as was also the tank and its walls. The reservoir which the tank really was, was a hollow in the centre of the floor, about four feet deep and about as many feet square. This was a hot spring which contained, no doubt, various mineral ingredients; but the water in the basin was perfectly clear and transparent, and tasteless and without odour as well, as some finding its way into the mouth testified. The spring is said to possess medical virtues, but I did not know for what kind of ailments, as I have not taken the trouble to find out. Nor was I subject to any chronic disease, and this phase of the matter had never occurred to me. Only a line of poetry that comes to me, every time I take a dip is that of the Chinese poet Pai Le-tien:

> "Soft and warm the water of the spring,
> All impurities are cleansed away."

A mention of a spring awakens in me the pleasant feeling which this couplet expresses, and I hold that no hot spring deserves to be called by that name unless it makes one feel that way. This is an ideal, apart from which I have no demand to make of any hot spring.

Clear up to a little under my chin the pleasant warm water in the tank reached and was indeed overflowing beautifully on all sides, without making it known where it was welling up from.

Resting my head, with face upward, on the back of my hands which held on to the slightly raised side of the tank, I let my body rise up to the point of least resistance and I felt my soul float buoyantly like the jellyfish. Life is easy in this state of existence. You unlock the door of prudence and cast all desires to the Four Winds, and become part of the hot water, leaving it completely to the hot water to make what it likes of you. The more floating, the less is the pain to live for that which floats. There will be more blessings than to have become a disciple of Jesus Christ, for one who lets even one's soul float. At this rate, even drowning is not without its picturesqueness. I have forgotten what piece, but I think I remember reading Swinburne, where the poet depicts a woman rejoicing in her eternal peaceful rest. Millais' *Ophelia*, which has ever been a source of sentimental uneasiness to me, offers also something aesthetic, when viewed in this light. Why he should have chosen so unpleasant a scene has always been a puzzle to me; but now I saw that it made an artistic production. A form, a figure, a look, floating in sweet painlessness, as it were, whether on the surface, or under water or floating and sinking, is indisputably aesthetic. With wild flowers judiciously sprinkled on the banks and the water, the floating one, and the floating one's dress, making a harmonious and well arranged ensemble of colours, it will without fail make a picture. But if the floating one's expression were nothing but peace itself, the picture would almost make only a mythology or an allegory, while convulsive pain will, on the other hand, destroy the whole effect. The expression of a naive and care-unknown face will not bring out human sentiments. What kind of a face should it be to be a success? Millais' *Ophelia* may be a success; but I doubt that he is one with me in spirit. However, Millais is Millais and I am I; and I feel like painting a person drowned. But I fancied that the face that I wanted would not easily come to me.

Buoying myself in the bath, I next tried to make poetry of the appreciation of the drowned:

> "Will get wet in rain,
> Will be cold in frost,
> Will be dark underground,
> On the wave when floating,
> Under the wave when sunk,
> Will be painless in warm Spring water."

It was raining outside, the soft, quiet, warm rain of Spring. The plaintive *twang, twang* of a samisen heard at a distance on a night like this is a peculiarly appealing sound, and it was catching my ear, as I was humming my extempore song of the drowned. Not that I pretend to know anything about this particular instrument of string music; in fact I am rather dubious about my ear being able to tell any difference of a higher or lower pitch of the second or third string. Nevertheless, with a gentle mercy-like rain putting me in this fame of mind, and even my soul lazily sporting in a delightfully pleasant warm bath, it gladdened my heart to hear floating music, with not a shadow of care within or without me.

The samisen awoke in me the long-forgotten memories of my boyhood days, when I used to go out into my father's garden and sit under three pine trees, to listen to O-Kura-san, the fair daughter of a sake shop on the other side of the street, sing and play a samisen on calm Spring afternoons.

I was lost in living over again the long past, when the door of the bath room opened. I thought somebody was coming in. Leaving my body buoyant, I turned my eyes only toward the entrance. I had my head resting on that part of the tank which was farthest from the entrance door, so that my eyes covered obliquely the steps leading downward, about seven yards away from me. Nothing as yet appeared before my uplifted eyes: my ears caught only the sound of the rain dropping from the eaves. The plaintive samisen had stopped I did not know when. Presently something appeared at the head of the steps. There was in the room a solitary small hanging oil lamp, which, even at its best, shed but scanty light, to make things clear in their colour; but what, with the rain outside shutting in the vapours, and the whole place filled with a cloud of mist, there could be no telling who it was coming down.

The dim figure carried its foot a step down; but one might have fancied that the step stone was velvety smooth and its stepping so noiseless that it could not have moved at all. The figure became clearer in outline, and an artist as I am, my perception of the build of a body is more accurate than you might have thought, so that, the moment it came a step down, I knew that I was alone with a woman in the bath room. The woman came fully in view before me as I was debating with myself whether I should or should not take any notice of her. The next moment I was lost to all but a beautiful vision. The figure gracefully straightened itself to its full height, with the soft light of the lamp playing about the warm light pink of the upper regions, over which hung a cloud of dark hair. The sight swept away from me all thoughts of formality, decorum and propriety, my only consciousness then being that I had before me a superbly beautiful theme.

Be the ancient Greek sculpture what it is, every time I see a nude picture, which modern French painters make their life of, I miss something in its unuttered power of impression, because of the voluptuous extremes to which effort is made in order to bring out the beauty of the flesh. This feeling has always been a source of mental uneasiness to me, as I could not answer myself exactly why, pictures of this class looked low in taste, as I think they do.

Cover the flesh, its beauty disappears; but uncovering makes it base. The modern art of painting the nude does not stop at the baseness of uncovering; but not content with merely reproducing the figure stripped of its clothing, would make the nude shoulder its way into the world of decorum and ceremony. Forgetting that being wrapped in clothes is the normal state of human life, they are trying to give the nude all the rights. They are striving to bring out strongly the fact of being stark-naked, emphasizing the point excessively, indeed, over-excessively beyond fullness. Art carried to this extreme debases itself, in proportion as it coerces one who looks at it. The beautiful begins, as a rule, to look the less beautiful, the more beautiful it is struggled to make it appear. This is precisely what, in human affairs, gives life to the proverb, "fullness is the beginning of waning."

Care-freeness and innocence generally present something comfortably in reserve, which latter is an indispensable condition in paintings as in literature. The great failing of modern art is its labouring in the mud, which the so-called tide of civilization is depositing everywhere. The painting of the nude is a good example of it. In Japanese cities are what are called the geisha, who traffc in their own beauty. These demi-mondes know not how to express themselves, but are concerned about how they may look in the eyes of those who come for their company. The yearly salon catalogues are full of pictures of the nude, who are like these geisha. They are not only unable to forget that they are naked, but they are bringing every muscle of their bodies into full play to show that they are nude.

Not a trace of all that pertains to this vulgar atmosphere was about the exquisitely beautiful vision before me. To say "being stripped of clothes" would be descending to the human level; but the vision before me was as natural as one called into life in a world of snow in the age of gods, when there was no clothes to wear, nor any sleeves to put hands through.

Cloud after cloud of vapour rolled and tumbled in the half transparent light, and a world of trembling rainbows hung in the midst of which rose a snow white form, shading upward into mistily black hair. Oh, that dreamy figure!

The two lines that inwardly met at the neck, slanted gracefully downward over the shoulders, and bent roundly ending in five tapering fingers. The plump chest heaving and unheaving sent its slow undulations downward and a pair of well-shaped feet, that supported the legs carrying the whole weight of the body, easily solved the complex problem of equipoise and gravitation, presenting a unity so natural, so gentle, and so free from constraint that the like could nowhere else be found.

Withal this figure stood before me, not thrust to view like the ordinary nude, but enveloped in an atmosphere that lends mystery to everything in it; only suggesting, so to speak, the profound loveliness of its beauty behind a thin veil. A few scales in a spread of inky cloud, make one see in fancy the horned monster of a dragon behind the canvas; such is the power of art and spirit behind it. The vision before me, was perfect, as art would have it in its atmosphere, geniality and phantasmality. If it be true that painting carefully six times six, thirty-six scales of a dragon can only end in a ludicrousness, there is a psychic charm in gazing not too clearly at the stark nakedness of a body. When the figure appeared before my eyes I fancied to see in it a heavenly maiden, fled from the moon, standing hesitatingly, being hard pressed by the chasing aurora.

The figure gradually rose out of the water, and I feared that a step more would make it a thing of this fallen world. But just in the nick of time, the black hair shook like a magician's wand calling for wind, and the snowy vision swept through the whirling cloud of steam and flew up the steps to the doorway. A moment later a woman's ringing chuckle sounded on the other side of the door, leaving dying echoes behind in the still quiet of the bath room. The agitated water of the tank washing over my face, I stood on my feet, and its waves beat me about my chest. The water overflowed from the bath with a noise.

VIII

I had tea, with a priest named Daitetsu, the abbot of Kaikanji temple, and a lay-youth of about twenty-four years, as my fellow-guests, and Nami-san's father, of course as mine host, in his own room. Nami-san is the name of the *O-Jo-san* of Shiota.

The room was one of about six mats, but looked rather small and narrow, with a large square short-legged rosewood table in the centre. The table stood partly on a Chinese rug and partly on a tiger skin, which together nearly filled the floor of the room. The youth and I squatted cross-legged on the rug, and the priest and the host on the skin. There was something undeniably continental in the rug, with a crazy sort of appearance in its figures, as is the case with most things Chinese. But that is where their value resides. You gaze at Chinese furniture and ornaments. You think they are dull or grotesque; but presently you become conscious that there is in that dullness or grotesqueness something that has a power of fascinating you irresistibly, and that is what makes them precious. Japan produces her art goods with the attitude of a pickpocket; and the West is large in scale and fine in execution, but inalterably worldly and practical. A train of thought of some such trend was coursing in me as I sat down, with the youth sharing the rug.

The tiger skin, on which the priest sat, had its tail stretched out near my knees, and its head under mine host, who seemed to have had all his grey hair pulled out of his head and planted in his cheeks and chin. Whiskers and beard were growing rampantly in a striking contrast to the shiny smoothness of his uppermost regions. He, the host, lay on the table tea things, not the paraphernalia for stiff ceremonial powdered tea drinking, but just for sipping clear green tea.

"We have a guest in the house—we haven't had one for quite a while—and I thought, we should have a quiet tea party...." said the old man turning toward the priest.

"Thank you for your invitation. I have not called on you for weeks, and was thinking I should come down to see you today." The priest looked about sixty years old, with a rotund face, that would do credit to a picture of Bodhidharma in a congenial mood. He seemed to be a friend of mine host of long standing.

"Is this gentleman your guest?"

Nodding his head in acknowledgment, the old gentleman took up a *kyusu* teapot and poured—no—permitted a few drops of yellowish green liquid to trickle, in turns, into four tea cups, producing faint echoes of pure sweet flavour on my olfactory organ.

"You must feel lonesome, alone in a country place like this?" The priest began to speak to me.

"Haa," I answered in a most equivocal sort of way; for a "yes" would have told a lie; but if I said "no," it would have required a long string of explanations.

"No, *Osho-san*," interposed my host "this gentleman has come out here for painting. He is even keeping himself busy."

"Oh, so, that is good. Of the Nanso school?"

"No, *Osho-san*," I replied this time. I thought he would not understand, if I said oil painting, and I did not say so.

"No," the old one again took it upon himself to complete information, "his is that oil painting."

"Ah, I see, the Western painting, which Kyuichi-san, here works at? I saw the kind, for the first time, in his production; it was very beautifully done."

The young one opened his mouth at length and most diffidently asserted that "It was a poor affair."

"You showed some of your stuff to *Osho-san*?" asked the old man. Judging by the tone in which this was said and the attitude assumed by the old one towards the young, they would seem to be relatives.

"No, it was only that I was caught painting by the *Osho-sama* at Kagamiga Ike pond, the other day."

"Hum, is that so? Well, here is a cup of tea for you," said the host, placing a cup each before his guests. There were a few drops of tea in, though the cups were quite large. They were dark grey in colour outside, with a yellowish picture or design on them, delightfully tasteful, but the name of their maker was quite undecipherable.

"It is Mokubey's," briefly explained the old gentleman.

"This is very interesting," I complimented briefly also.

"There are many imitations in Mokubeys. These have the inscription; look at the base," says the host.

I took up my cup and held it towards the semitransparent shoji. On the screen was seen a potted *haran* plant casting its shadow warmly. I looked into the base twisting my head, and saw there "Mokubey" burnt in diminutively. Inscriptions are not indispensables for real connoisseurs; but amateurs seem, generally, very sensitively particular about them. I brought the cup to my lips, instead of putting it back on the table. Leisurely lovers of real good tea rise to the seventh heaven, when, drop, drop, they let the correctly drawn aromatic liquid roll on the tip of their tongues. Ordinarily, people think that tea is to be drunk; but that is not correct. A drop on your tongue; something refreshing spreads over it, you have practically nothing more to send down your throat, except that a delightfully soothing flavour travels down the alimentary canal into the stomach. It is vulgar to bring the teeth to service; but pure fresh water is too light. Gyokuro tea is thicker than water, but not heavy enough for the molar action. It is a fine beverage. If the objection be that tea robs one of sleep, then I should say "better be without sleep than be without tea." In the midst of my usual philosophical musing, the priest spoke to me again.

"Can you paint in oil on fusuma?[43] If you can, I should like to have some painted."

If the priest would have me do it, I may not refuse; but that it would please him was not at all certain, and I should hate to retire crestfallen, by having it declared that an oil painting is no good, after I had spared no labour for its execution.

"I do not think oil paintings will go well on a fusuma."

"You do not think so? You are probably right. What I have seen of Kyuichi-san's production will make me think that it will look perhaps too gay on a fusuma."

"Mine is no good. It was an idle piece of work," says the youth with a stress on his words, apologetically and abashedly.

"Where is that what-do-you-call-it pond?" I asked the youth for my information.

"In the hollow of valley just in the rear of Kaikanji temple. It is a quiet lonely place. That picture.... I took lessons in school... I just tried it to while away the time."

"And that Kaikanji?"

"Kaikanji is the name of a temple in my charge. It is a fine place, with the sea stretching from right under you. You must come and see me, while you are here. It is not more than a mile from here. From that verandah... there you can see its stone steps."

"Won't I make myself unwelcome by calling on you any time to please myself?"

"Decidedly not; you will always find me in. *O-Jo-san* of this house pays me visits quite often. Speaking of the *O-Jo-san*, O-Nami-san does not seem to be around, today. Anything the matter with her, Shiota-san?"

"Has she gone out? Has she been your way, Kyuichi?"

"No, uncle; we haven't seen her around."

"Out on one of her solitary walks, again, perhaps. Ha, ha, ha. O-Nami-san is pretty strong-legged. A clerical business took me down to Tonami the other day. About Sugatami bridge I thought I saw one very like her, and it was she. She almost sprang on me, taking me by surprise, with one of her outbursts: 'Why are you dragging along, so, *Osho-san*? Where are you going?'

She was in her pair of straw sandals, with her skirt tucked up. 'Where have you been in that attire?' I asked her. 'I have been picking marsh-parsley; you shall have some.' Saying this, she took out a handful of unwashed mud-covered plants and pushed it down my sleeve. Ha, ha, ha."

"That girl did!" said that girl's father with one of the grimmest of smiles, and seized the first opportunity to change the topic, by taking down from rosewood book case something heavy looking in a damask silk bag. He informed us that the bag contained an ink-stone, that once belonged to Rai Sanyo, as one of desk stationeries most treasured by that famous poet-historian and scholar-calligrapher of generations ago. This naturally led to a critical discussion of autographs of Shunsui, Kyohei, Sanyo, Sorai, etc. The ink-stone brought to view at last drew forth admiration from the priest, who was infatuated with the "eyes" and the irridescent colour of the stone. It went without saying that the ink-stone was originally imported from China.

"A stone like this must be rare even in China, Shiota-san?"

"Yes."

"I should like to have one like this. May I ask you to get me one, Kyuichi-san?" ventured the abbot.

"He, he, he, I might be killed before I found one," retorted the youth.

"Hoi, I am forgetting, it is no time to talk of getting an ink-stone and things of that kind. By the by, when do you start?"

"I leave here in a few days, *Osho-sama.*"

"You should go down to Yoshida, to see him off, old man."

"I am getting on in years and ordinarily I should excuse myself. But this time we may part never to meet again, and I am resolved to go down to see him off."

"No, uncle, you must not take trouble to go down to Yoshida for me."

I now felt sure that the youth was really a nephew of mine host. I even saw some resemblance between them.

"You must not say so. You should let your uncle see you off. A river-boat will take him down there in no time. Isn't that so Shiota-san?"

"Yes. Crossing the mountain will be some job, but by taking a boat, though a little detour...."

The youth did not decline this time; but remained silent.

"Are you going to China?" I ventured to ask.

"Yes."

The monosyllable left me musing that he might not be the worse for a few more; but I felt no particular necessity to dig, and I held my peace. I noticed that the shadow of *haran* had changed its position.

"Well, gentleman, you see the present war—he was formerly with the colours in one year service—and he has been called out to join his old regiment."

My old host volunteered in his nephew's place to let me understand that the youth was destined to leave for Manchuria in a day or two. I had thought that there was only feathered songsters to listen to, only flowers to see fall, only hot spring to warble forth in this dreamy land of poetry in a mountain bosom, in peaceful Spring. Alas, the living world had come crossing the sea and mountain and oozing into this home of a forgotten tribe, and the time may come when a small fraction of blood making a crimson sea of bleak Manchuria may flow from this youth's arteries. This very youth is sitting next to an artist who sees nothing worth seeing in human life but dreaming. He sits so near that the artist may hear his heart throb. In that throb may be resounding even now, the tide rolling high in a plain hundreds of miles away. Fate has accidentally brought these two together in a room, but tells nothing else, nor gives the reason why.

IX

"Studying?" asked a woman's voice outside my door. On returning to my room, I took out one of the books I had brought, tied to my tripod, and was reading it.

"Go right ahead, Sensei, don't mind me," said the voice before I gave any answer, and its owner walked right into my room with no conventionality whatever.

A shapely neck, looking all the more fair because of the subdued colour of the part of kimono protecting its lower half, it was this charming contrast that struck my eye, as the woman sat before me.

"A foreign book? Full of hardy, knotty problems, I suppose, Sensei?"

"No, not quite."

"Then, what is it all about?"

"Well, to be honest, I do not know well enough to tell you."

"Ho, ho, ho, and yet you are studying?"

"I am not studying. I put it on the desk, open it at random, and just skim the open page. That is all."

"Does that sort of thing interest you?"

"Marvellously."

"How?"

"How? Why, that is the most interesting way of reading novels."

"You are so odd, Sensei."

"Yes, I should say I am rather."

"Why should you not read them from the beginning?"

"If you begin to read from the beginning, you will have to read to the end, don't you see?"

"How absurdly you talk. There can be nothing wrong in reading through a novel?"

"No, of course not. If it is to read the plot, I, also shall do so."

"What else is there to read, if not the plot?"

She is after all a woman, I thought, and felt like testing her.

"Do you like novels?"

"I?" She made a pause after the word, and then said ambiguously: "Well in a way." She seemed not to care much about novel-reading.

"Perhaps you are not sure yourself that you like or you do not like reading-novels?"

"What difference does it make if one likes or not likes novels?" Novels seemed to have no claim to existence in her mind.

"It would not matter, then, if one read them from the beginning or from the end, or from any page one happened to open. I should think, you need not be so curious about my way of reading."

"But you and I are different."

"In what way, please." I looked into the woman's eyes, thinking, I was testing her. But they spoke nothing.

"Ho, ho, ho, you don't see?"

"But you must have read a good many in your younger days?" I made a little detour, instead of keeping straight to my point.

"I am still young—at least in heart—you unkind man." The falcon I let off was once more going astray to miss the prey: she would let me have no chance. But I managed to bring her back on the track by retorting: "Being able to say that sort of thing in the face of a man, you must be counted among the not young."

"Arn't you, who say that, also well up in age? And you mean to say that you still delight in reading of love, Cupid and all that kind of trash?"

"Yes, they are delightful and will not cease to interest me even till my last hour."

"Well I declare! That is how you can give yourself up to a profession like yours, I suppose?"

"Precisely so. Because I am an artist, I have no need to read through novels from the beginning to the end. But they interest me no matter what part I read. It delights me to talk with you, so much so that I should be glad to be all the time talking with you, while I am here. If you would have it, I have not the slightest objection, on my part, to falling incandescently, in love with you. That would be most interesting. But, however intensely in love, there is no need that we should become husband and wife. One must need read through novels from the beginning to the end, as long as one feels the necessity of love ending in a marriage."

"The artist is, then, he who makes an inhuman love?"

"Not inhuman but unhuman. The plots of novels do not count at all, because we read them unhumanly. You see, I open the book thus, as in a lottery drawing, and I read the first page that lies flat before me. And there is the charm of the thing."

"That does sound interesting. Then I wish you would tell me something of what you are reading. I should like to know how interesting it really is."

"To tell you would not do. Don't you see, the charm of a picture would all be gone, if you simply made a narration of it."

"Ho, ho, ho, read it to me, then, please."

"In English?"

"No, in Japanese."

"It would be a job to read English in Japanese."

"It would be lovely, being so unhuman."

A fun for the while, I thought, and began to read the book in Japanese, with stops and pauses. If there was an unhuman way of reading, mine was certainly it, and the woman was listening also unhumanly.

"'An aura of tenderness rose from the woman—from her voice, from her eyes, from her skin. The woman went to the stern helped by the man. Did she go there to have a look at Venice, now enshrouded in the evening dusk? And the man, did he help her to feel lightning flashes in his blood on his side?'—Mind, it is all unhuman, and don't look for accuracy. I may make skips, too."

"I won't mind a bit, Sensei; you may add in something of your own if you like."

"'The woman was leaning against the gunwale by the side of the man, with a distance between them narrower than her ribbons, which the wind was playing with. The Doge of Venice was now vanishing in light red like the second sunset....'"

"What is the Doge, Sensei?"

"It doesn't matter what that means. However, it is the name of the man who long ago ruled over Venice. I don't know how many Doges succeeded one another. Anyhow their palace has outlived them and may still be seen in Venice."

"Who are that man and woman?"

"God only knows, and that is why it is so interesting. You need not bother yourself about what their relations have been. I find them together just like you and I here. There is something interesting, don't you see, just for the occasion?"

"As you please. They seem to be in a boat."

"On land or in water, it is just as it is written. You will make a detective of yourself, if you press for 'why.'"

"Ho, ho, ho, I will not ask you then."

"Ordinary novels are all inventions of detectives and denuded of unhumanity they are all so insipid."

"Good, then, tell me more of unhumanity. What follows next, please?"

"'Venice is sinking, sinking to a faint single streak of line. The line dwindles into dots. Here and there pillars stand in an opal sky, last of all the highest towering belfry sinks. It has sunk, says the friend. The woman, who has come away from Venice is free like the wind of the sky in her heart. But the thought that she must come back to Venice, which has disappeared, fills her heart with the anguish of bondage. The man and woman direct their eyes toward the darkening bay. The stars are increasing. The sea is softly undulating without any foam. The man took the woman's hand in his, feeling like one holding a bowstring that has not yet stopped vibrating.'"

"That does not seem to sound very unhuman."

"But you can hear it as unhuman. If you don't like it, I shall skip a little."

"Oh, no, I am all right."

"If you are all right, why, I am a great deal more all right. Now, let me see—it is getting so bungling—it is so awkward to trans—I mean, to read."

"You may cut it out, if it be so bothering."

"No, I shall go it rough—'This one night, says the woman. One night? asks the man. Say, many, many nights; it is heartless to limit it to a single night.'"

"Who says that, the man or the woman?"

"The man, O-Nami-san, I think the woman does not want to go back to Venice, and the man is saying this to console her—'In the memory of the man, who lay down on the midnight deck with his head on a coil of halyard, that instant—an instant like a hot drop of blood—that instant in which he tightly held the woman's hand in his, tossed like a great wave. Looking up into the black night, he resolved, come what may, to save the woman from the brink of forced marriage. With his mind made up, he closed his eyes....'"

"The woman?"

"'Lost on the road, the woman seemed not to know whither she was wandering. Like a man sailing in the sky a captive, unfathomable mystery....'—the rest is so awkward to read, you see, it does not complete the sentence—'only the unfathomable mystery'—isn't there any verb?"

"Never mind a verb. Sensei, you don't want any verb; that is quite enough."

"Eh?"

All of a sudden a rumbling sound came, and all the trees on the mountain spoke. We looked at each other, not knowing why, and saw a solitary spray of camellia in a small vessel on my desk swinging.

"An earthquake!" Nami-san brought herself right up against my desk, with a break in her pose, as she said this, and our bodies were oscillating, almost touching each other. A pheasant—a bird credited with superhuman sensitiveness for seismic phenomena—flew out of the bamboo bush, making a sharp noise with the flapping of its wings.

"A pheasant," I said looking out of the window.

"Where?" said the woman with another break in her posture, bringing herself closer to me. She was so near me that our heads were almost in contact with each other. I felt on my moustaches breaths coming out of her gentle nostrils.

"Remember, all unhumanity!" said the woman unequivocally as she quickly corrected her pose.

"Of course," I responded promptly.

A pool of water in the hollow of a rock in the garden was agitating in alarm; but that body of water moving from the very bottom as a whole, there was no break in the surface but irregular curves. If there be such an expression as moving "full roundly," it fitted exactly, I thought, the condition of this pool of water. A wild cherry tree, which had its shadow cast peacefully in the pool, now stretched out of all shape, now shrivelled up, then wriggled and twisted. For all those contortions, it was most interesting to observe that the tree never failed to appear the cherry tree it was.

"This is delightful. There is beauty and variation. Motion must be of this sort to be interesting."

"Man will be all right as long as his motion is of this sort, no matter how hard he moves."

"You cannot move like this unless you are unhuman."

"Ho, ho, ho, how deeply in love you are with unhumanity, Sensei!"

"Nor can you deny that you are not without partiality for it, after your bridal gown show yesterday?" I made a lunge.

She parried by saying sweetly with a coquettish smile: "A nice reward please."

"What for, my young lady?"

"You wished to see, and so I took the trouble to get up the show for you."

"I wished?"

"A Sensei of painting who had come up crossing the mountain, took the trouble, I am told, to ask the old woman of a humble tea house on the mountain pass to let him see me in my wedding gown."

This came so unexpectedly that I was out of a ready answer. Nor did the woman give me any chance, she quickly came down on me:

"All obliging, however sincere, can only be lost on a man so forgetful," came in mocking reproach, like a frontal blow. I was beginning to get the worst of it, being at her mercy, unable to catch up with the start she had of me.

"That bath tank show, last night, was then, also out of your kindness?" I narrowly managed to regain my ground.

She made no reply.

"A thousand pardons for being so ungrateful. What would you command of me in penance?" I went forward as far as I could in anticipation; but in vain. She kept on looking up to the framed calligraphy of the priest, Daitetsu, as if she saw and heard nothing. Presently she read it in a soft murmur:

"Shadow of bamboo sweeping no dust rises." Now she turned right round to me and said as if she suddenly came back to herself:

"What did you say, Sensei?"

She said it with a studied loudness; but I was not to be caught.

"I met that priest a while ago." I set myself in motion for her benefit, imitating the "full round" movement of the earthquake shaken pool of water.

"The *Osho-san* of Kaikanji? He is quite stout, isn't he?"

"He asked me if I would paint in oil on his paper screen! Those Zen priests are full of absurdities, arn't they?"

"Probably that is why they get so fat."

"I also met another, a young man."

"Kyuichi, you mean."

"Yes Kyuichi-san."

"You seem to know so well."

"No, I know Kyuichi-san only by name, but nothing else about him. He seems to hate moving his lips."

"No, he is little shy, that is all. He is a mere boy."

"A boy? Isn't he of about the same age as you?"

"Ho, ho, ho, you think so? He is a cousin of mine. He is going to the front, and came to say goodbye."

"Is he stopping here?"

"No, he is staying with my brother."

"I see. He came to take a cup of tea, then?"

"He likes ordinary hot water better than tea. But my father would have him. Poor thing, he must have had a hard half hour of it. I would have let him go before the party rose, if I were there."

"Where have you been? The priest was asking after you—if you were out again on one of your lonely walks?"

"Yes, I was. I made a round of Kagamiga Ike pond and neighbourhood."

"I should myself like to go and see that pond."

"Do, by all means, Sensei."

"Will it make a good picture?"

"It is a good place for drowning yourself."

"I have no idea of ending my life in water for some time to come."

"I may, before long."

Too bold a joke for a woman, and I looked up into her eyes. She seemed quite sound, more herself than I expected.

"Won't you paint for me, Sensei, a picture of myself, drowned and floating in water—not struggling and in agony—but a nice little picture of me floating in easy, painless eternal repose."

"Eh?"

"Thunder and lightning, you are astonished?"

Nami-san got to her feet lightly and three steps brought her to the opening of my room. She turned back and threw at me the most innocent of her smiles, as she walked out of it. For a long time I sat immobile as one lost in reverie.

X

My curiosity brought me, the next day, to the Kagamiga Ike, a pool of water, not more than half a mile in circumference, by an actual survey, but looking immeasurably larger, when seen through openings in the brushwood, embowering its zigzag water-edge. I left it to my feet to take me where they liked, and I stopped when they came to a halt at a spot close to and falling into water, determined not to move till I got sick of it. Lucky that I could indulge in a whim like this; for in Tokyo I would be run over by a tram car, if not sternly chased away by a policeman. Ah! the city is a place where they make a beggar of a peaceful citizen, and pay a high salary to detectives who are all but boss pickpockets!

I sat on a damp cushion, which I found in incipient Spring grass, satisfied that I was in the bosom of nature, where neither wealth nor power could disturb me, and where I could heartily laugh at the folly of Timon's wrath. I then took out and lighted a cigarette, and as a streak of smoke from the match took the shape of a dragon with its tail tapering to a line, and vanished in a moment, I drew nearer to the water edge. I looked into the clear and placid water of the pond and saw some slender weeds reposing as in eternal peace in its not necessarily unfathomable depth. Unlike the shear grass on the bank which moved in the breeze, the weeds down in the bottom were doomed, I fancied, never to stir till their surrounding water moved in ripples, an event, which in all appearance, seemed never to come. Possessed of willingness to be animate, but imprisoned in the watery dungeon, they appeared to have been waiting in vain, morning after morning, and evening after evening, for an opportunity to be sported with, and eking out a life of forced immobility, unable to die. I picked up a couple of pebbles and dropped one of them into the water. I saw a couple or three of the thin stalks of weeds move wearily, as some bubbles came up to the surface; but the next moment more bubbles hid them from sight, as if they must not be seen in motion. I threw in the other pebble, with some force this time; but the poor resigned thing would not respond to my efforts to awaken them, and I left the place and walked a little way up the slow incline.

A huge tree stood over my new position of vantage, screening me from the sun and making me feel chilly. Near the water's edge, on the other side of the pond, was an overhanging camellia tree in full bloom. There is something very heavy and dull in the green of camellia leaves, even when seen in the sunshine, and I would have never known this particular plant but for its blood red flowers, which are never attractive, though fiery and striking. I never look at camellia flowers in a deep forest or mountain without wishing that I had not seen them; their red is not a common red, but a red with something weird in it like a she-demon in a fair woman's mask, who fascinates you with her black eyes and beauty and breathes poison into your pores before you know it. The pear blossoms in rain never fail to arouse a sentiment of pity; the aronia in pale moon light awakens love; but the camellia's cheerless red bespeaks a dark poison and something ominous.

As I was looking at those dark red flowers, as if under a spell, one of them fell into the water below, absolutely the only thing in motion in the still Spring day. Presently another dropped. The eerie thing about the camellia flower is that it never breaks up when it falls, as do most other flowers, but keeps compactly together, never to let its secret out, as it were. But one more fell, followed by another, after an interval, by still another, and still another, like the minute gun. Surely, I thought, the whole surface of the pond would turn red, by and by. I fancied the water looked slightly reddish already where the flowers were floating. Would they ever sink? Their red would melt, they would rot, become mud and fill up the pool, until there would be no more Kagamiga Ike, but a dry land after thousands of years. Hoy! one more extra-big blood red flower fell, and drop, drop, drop, followed by others, never ceasing to pass into eternity.

I now became seized with a queer idea, how it would look to paint a pond like this, with a beautiful woman floating in its water. I went back to the spot where I first stopped and there continued to think on the imaginary picture. Then with a tingling sensation, rushed back to my memory, the joking remark of Nami-san of the hot spring hotel, yesterday, that she should like to have me paint her dead, but floating with a pleasant face in the water. Suppose, I thought, I made her float in the water under that camellia. I wondered if I could make my brush tell that the blood red flowers were forever dropping, dropping, dropping into the water on her, and she was forever lying in her watery bed, in her eternal peaceful repose. But it was no easy matter, I told myself, to give expression to the idea of superhuman eternity, without rising above the level of mortal humanity.

Besides, the greatest difficulty lay in the choice of the face. Nami-san, with her usual expression of a discordant mixture of derision, impetuosity and soft heart, would never do, I thought. The face must bear no trace of mental or physical agony; but one with effulgent lightheartedness would be worse. Perhaps I had better borrow another woman's face; but the racking of my head revealed to me none to fit my imaginary picture, so that I felt that it must be Nami-san, after all. Yet there was something lacking in her to suit my purpose, and the tantalising part of it was how to make up for that something, it being impossible to work my whilom fancy into it to fill up what was lacking. How would it do to give the face a touch of jealousy? But that would make it look too uneasy. How about hatred, then? That would again be too strong. Anger? No, it would spoil the whole effect. Resentment for some particular cause is sometimes poetical and acceptable; but as an every day feeling, it is too commonplace.

I thought and thought and thought, and it suddenly flashed upon me that what was missing from Nami-san was pity and compassion. Compassion is a feeling unknown to the gods, and yet is one that makes man as near gods as possible. This was one sentiment which I had never yet seen reflected in Nami-san, and I was convinced that my picture would become an accomplished fact, the moment I saw it aroused by some impulse or other and flashed across her handsome face. For the moment, however, I had absolutely no idea as to when or if ever, I should have the good fortune to see it in her.

A bantering sort of smile and a knitted brow bespeaking an eager desire to get the better of you are the ever constant features of her face and nothing can be done with them only. Hark! A rustling sound as of somebody wading through dry leaves came, and the mental plan of my picture, two-thirds of which I had finished forming went to pieces. Looking up, I saw a man in tight sleeved kimono, loaded with some faggots on his back, coming through the creeping bamboo growths towards the Kaikanji, apparently from the neighbouring hill.

"Fine weather, Sir," said the man to me, taking off a towel from his head. He made a bow, and as he did so, a flash from a sharpened hatchet, stuck in his belt, caught my eyes. He was a sturdily built men of about forty, with a face I remembered seeing somewhere. He spoke to me familiarly:

"*Danna* paints, too?" I had my colour-box open by me.

"Yes, I have come out here, thinking I might make a picture of this pond. This is a very lonely place; nobody comes round."

"Yes, it is very much in the mountain.... *Danna*, you had a time of it in rain, on that pass. I am sure, it was a bad toiling along you had that time."

"Eh? why, yes, you are the *mago-san* I saw, then?"

"Yes. I gather faggots as you see and take them down to the town to sell." Gembey took his load down from his back and sat on it. His hand brought out a tobacco pouch, a very ancient affair, that refused to tell whether it was of leather or of imitation leather. I gave him a lighted match and said:

"It must be a great job for you to cross a place like that, every day?"

"No, *Danna*, I am used to it. Besides I don't do it every day, but only once in three days, and sometimes four days."

"For myself, I should be excused even for once in four days."

"Aha, ha, ha, ha. It is hard on my pony, and I generally make it four days or so."

"That is, you think more of your horse than yourself, eh? Ha, ha, ha, ha!"

"Not quite that...."

"By the way, this pond looks very old. Have you any idea, how old it is?"

"This has been here from olden times."

"From olden times? How old?"

"Well, from a very long time ago."

"From a very long time ago, I see."

"A very long time ago, anyway, from the time when the *Jo-sama* of Shiota threw herself into it."

"Shiota? That spa-hotel you mean?"

"Yes."

"You say the *O-Jo-san* drowned herself here? But she is alive, very much alive there?"

"No, not that *Jo-sama*, but a *Jo-sama* of long, long ago."

"Long, long ago? About when?"

"Well, a *Jo-sama* of very great long ago...."

"What made that *Jo-sama* of so long ago throw herself into water?"

"That *Jo-sama* was, it is said, as beautiful as the present *Jo-sama*, *Danna-sama*."

"Yes?"

"One day there came along a *bonroji*...."

"*Bonroji?* You mean that begging minstrel that used to come round of old, playing his shakuhachi pipe?"

"Yes, that shakuhachi *bonroji*. While this *bonroji* was stopping at Squire Shiota's house, the beautiful *Jo-sama* took a fancy to him. Would you call it fate or what? Anyhow, she said she must have him, and cried."

"Cried? You don't say!"

"But the Squire would not have a *bonroji* for his son-in-law, and drove away the party."

"Drove away the *bonroji*?"

"Yes. The *Jo-sama* ran out of the house after him, and coming here, she threw herself into the water from where that yonder pine tree is standing. The whole place went into an awful excitement then. It is said that the young *Jo-sama* had, at the time, a mirror with her, and the pond has since come to be called Kagamiga Ike. We still call this the Mirror Pond."

"Oh, the pond has made a grave, already, at least for one person?"

"A very scandalous affair, indeed."

"This was about how many Squires back, do you know?"

"It is said to be a very long time back, and... it is between you and I, *Danna-san*."

"What?"

"Every generation has had its mad one born in that Shiota family."

"Oh?"

"A curse must be on that house. They are all saying that the present *Jo-sama* is getting queer of late."

"Ha, ha, ha, ha. That seems improbable."

"You don't think so? But let me tell you that her mother had a touch of it, too."

"Is the old lady there?"

"No, she died last year."

"Hum," I said, looking at a thin cord of smoke rising from live tobacco ashes, Gembey emptied on the ground, and then closed my mouth. The man went away with the faggots on his back.

I had come out on my unhuman tour to do some painting. But what with my thinking and musing, what with being made to listen to old tales, I knew there would be no picture, no matter how many days I might be at it. This very day I was at the pond with my colour-box and tripod, and I thought I owed it to myself to make a picture of the place, somehow or other. I sat on my tripod and began to make a visual survey of the pool and its surroundings, to make up my mind, on how much of the scenery I should take into my picture. I knew my materials were pine trees, giant-leaved creeping bamboos, rocks and a mirror-like pool of water.

The question was, how much of them should be covered in my canvas. The creeping bamboos were growing quite close to the edge of the water, and some of the rocks were ten feet high, while the pine trees were scraping the sky and cast their shadows into the water far and long, so much so that I could not see how I might take them all on my canvas. I had half made up my mind that I should paint only the reflections of the waters in the pond, feeling almost certain that the novel idea would astonish the people. But then the astonishment must be one arising from the sense of admiration and appreciation for the substantial artistic value of the production. How to solve this part of the problem occupied my attention next. Naturally, my eyes directed themselves, to the reflections in the pond.

Strangely enough no definite picture would come from the study of shadows only, and it was irresistible that I should try to make something by following the watery reflections back to their originals on land. My eyes were closely studying the ten foot rock, from its lowest point in the water to its body above, when I felt myself under the spell of a fairy's wand, just as they had travelled to the summit of the cliff. I saw there a face in the struggling rays of setting sun that stole through the leafy screen and were faintly falling on the darkish top of the rock, the face of the woman, who had surprised me as a midnight shadow, or a vision, who had surprised me in her wedding gown, and had surprised me outside the bathroom! My eyes refused to turn elsewhere, as if rooted to the centre of the pale face of the woman who was standing fixedly on the rock, gently straightening herself up to her full height. Oh! that instant! I jumped on my feet. But the apparition had vanished, nimbly hopping down the other side of the rock and as she did so, I thought I perceived something red which resembled the camellia in her sash. The declining sun, slanting closely over tree tops, was faintly dyeing the trunks of the great pines, and below the creeping bamboos looked greener than ever. I was once more taken by surprise.

XI

That night I gave myself up to renewing my acquaintance with the priest, Daitetsu, by calling on him at Kaikanji temple, at the top of the stone steps. The old priest received me, not effusively but with a most cordial welcome.

"I am glad you have come. You must find life very tedious in these parts?"

"The beautiful moon lured me out for a walk, and my feet brought me here, to be plain, *Osho-san.*"

"Yes, the moon is beautiful tonight."

The priest said this as he slid open the front shoji of his chamber. The garden outside had nothing in it but two stepping stones and a single pine tree; but beyond extended a stretch of sea, dimly visible in the moonlight, with fishermen's lights innumerably dotting the watery surface as far as the horizon, where they seemed to change into stars.

"What a beautiful view, *Osho-san.* Isn't it a pity that you should keep it shut out?"

"True; but don't you see, it is not new to me, it being there before me every night?"

"I should never be tired of looking over a view like this. I should give up my sleep to be looking at it the whole night."

"Ha, ha, ha, you are an artist and different from an old priest like me."

"But *Osho-san*, you are not the less an artist, as long as you see the beautiful and enjoy it."

"That is so, though my artistic skill does not rise above drawing an apology of Bodhidharma. Speaking of Bodhidharma, you see a picture of the holy man in the niche there; it is from the brush of my predecessor, here. Pretty good, isn't it?"

True enough, there was a hanging picture of Bodhidharma which had absolutely no claim to any artistic value, except that it was a very innocent production, which gave no evidence of trying to hide the artist's want of skill.

"Why, it is artlessly good."

"There need be no more about pictures that our kind make. We are well satisfied as long as they represent our spirit."

"They are far better than pictures that bespeak skill but breathe base vulgarity."

"Ha, ha, ha, you know how to praise things. By the by is there the degree of Doctor for painters, these days?"

"No, *Osho-san*, there is no Doctor of Painting."

"You see I am so far away from civilization and know nothing of the latest novelties. I haven't been in Tokyo not even once in the last twenty years."

"You have missed nothing, *Osho-san*. It is all noise and nothing else in Tokyo."

The priest treated me to a good cup of tea, and then went on to ask:

"You seem to go about a great deal. Do you do so all for the purpose of painting?"

"Well, I carry about with me my painting outfit; but I am not at all particular about the actual painting itself."

"So? Can it be, then, that you are travelling and sojourning for the pleasure of doing so?"

"Well, you might say so. But the fact is I can't stand the life in Tokyo. They begin to sniff about you, when you have lived there any length of time."

"That is strange. Can it be for sanitary purposes?"

"No, *Osho-san*, it is the detective that does it."

"Detectives? The police then? The police stations and policemen, must there be such things?"

"They are useless, at least, to artists."

"Nor are they of any good to me. I have never had any occasion to be taken care of by them."

"I do not doubt you."

"For that matter I don't see why you should take their sniffng so much to heart. If I were you I would let them do all the sniffng they want. Even the police won't bother you as long as you keep straight. My predecessor used to tell me that a man must be able to make a clean breast of everything within him in broad daylight at Nihonbashi, the centre of Tokyo, and to find nothing to be ashamed of in it. Till then, he cannot be said to have finished his culture. You, my young friend, should strive to reach that stage of culture. Then you shall have no need of fleeing from Tokyo."

"You can rise to that height as soon as you shall have become a true artist."

"You had become one, then."

"But the police sniffng is more than I can bear."

"There, there, you are at it again. Look at that Nami-san of the hot spring hotel. She was tormented by all kinds of worrying thoughts on coming home to her father after being divorced from her husband, until she at last came to me, asking me, to free her from her mental anguish. I have been training her in the holy teaching, and she is now mastering herself wonderfully. You have seen yourself what a highly rational young woman she is."

"Yes, yes, I have thought she is a woman of no ordinary culture, *Osho-san*."

"Indeed, she is not. A few years ago I had under me a young disciple named Taian. She saved him from walking off the narrow path, and he is now on a fair way to attain high priesthood."

XII

It was Oscar Wilde, if I remember right, who said that Jesus of Nazareth was highly possessed of an artist's gifts. I do not know much about Christ; but I shall not hesitate to pronounce that the priest, Daitetsu of Kaikanji, is full well-qualified for an appreciation of this kind. Not that he takes much interest in art, nor that he is well versed in such things. He is enviably content with a production which can hardly be called a picture, and is innocent enough to think that there should be the Doctor of Painting! Nevertheless, he is well-qualified to be an artist. He is like a bag without a bottom: everything passes through him freely. No impurities stagnate within him. Only give him a touch of humour, and he shall be at home with everything he comes across, everywhere he goes, and will thus make a perfect artist.

As for myself, I shall never be a true artist as long as I cannot get over my annoyance with being sniffed at by detectives. I may sit before my easel and take up my palette, but that will not make me an artist. I can assume myself to be a real artist only when I come to a mountainous countryside like Nakoi and drink full of the joys of Spring. Once in this state of emancipation, all the beauties of nature become mine and I have made myself a first-class artist, even though I may not paint the smallest picture. I may not equal Michelangelo in art and take my hat off to Raphael in skill; but I acknowledge no inferiority in me by the side of the great masters of the past and present in the personality of an artist. I have not painted a single picture since I came here. I may look to have brought with me my colour-box, merely to satisfy a whim, and people may laugh at me as an imitation. Let them laugh; I am none the less a real artist, a sterling artist. It is not that one on this psychological height necessarily produces great works; but I hold that an artist who can turn out a worthy painting must have passed through that stage.

Thus I thought as I drew at a cigarette after breakfast. The sun had mounted high above the haze, and I saw the green of the trees standing out in relief with uncommon clearness in the back mountain when I opened the shoji.

The relations of air, and objects with colour are to me always the most interesting study in this universe. Work out atmosphere by giving first importance to colour, or let air be subordinate to the object, or weave colour and objects into atmosphere, all kinds of tune may be given to a picture, each depending upon a delicate variation in treatment. It goes without saying that this tune shows differently according to the particular tastes and fancies of individual artists, just as it is natural that it is influenced by time and place. There was never, for instance, a bright picture of scenery, painted by an Englishman. It may be that they are not fond of bright pictures; but even if they are, they cannot do anything with the atmosphere they have in England. Goodall is an Englishman; but the tune of colour is quite different in his productions. He never took any scenery in his own country for his theme. He chose for his picture the scenery of Egypt or Persia, where the atmosphere is much clearer than in England. Those who see his paintings for the first time wonder how an Englishman could bring out colours so clearly; so brightly are they all finished.

As for individual taste, there can be no help for it. However, if it be our object to paint Japanese scenery, we must work out a colour and atmosphere peculiar to Japan. French paintings are good; but you cannot call it a picture of Japanese scenery which is produced by simply copying their colours. You must come in contact with nature on the spot, studying, morning and evening, the shape and colour of the clouds, the shade of haze, etc., being ever prepared to go out with your tripod, the moment you see a colour which you think just right. Colour in nature is to be seen but momentarily, and once missed the same colour will not be easily caught again. The mountain I was looking at was full of a colour which was a rare good fortune for an artist to come across. I could not afford to miss it, and I started to go into the mountain to make a copy of it.

I left my room through a side fusuma way and stepped out into the verandah. The same moment my eyes caught the figure of Nami-san, leaning against the verandah railing, a little distance from me. Just as I began to call to her a word of greeting, she allowed her left hand to drop. No sooner had this happened when I saw something flash in her right hand and travel quickly two or three times over her chest, and then disappear as suddenly with a clap. The next instant she raised her left hand with a sheathed dagger in it. The show was over and phantom vanished behind a shoji. I wended my way to my sketching, thinking I had been given a morning treat in a theatrical rehearsal.

I walked upward slowly and as I did so the thought of Nami-san again possessed me. The first thing that occurred to me was that she would make a fine star if she went on the stage. Most actors and actresses assume visiting manners when before the footlights; but with Nami-san, her home is her stage and she is always acting, without knowing it. With her acting is natural. It may be that hers is what may be called an aesthetic life. Indeed life would be unbearable, with its constant surprises and alarms, if one did not accept hers as theatrical acting. She would soon make you dislike her, with her impulsive excesses, if you were to study her from the ordinary viewpoint of the novelist, with the commonplace background of duty, humanity, etc.

Suppose entangling relations of some sort grew up between her and myself; my mental agony would, I fancied, be then indescribable. I had come out on my present sojourn, I told myself, to be away from the "madding crowd," and to make of myself a confirmed artist. Everything that came to me through my two windows must, therefore, be seen as a picture. I must not set my eyes on any woman but that I saw in her a figure or character in a Noh play, a drama, or poetry. Seen through this psychological glass, I must say that of all the women I had ever met, Nami-san was the one who acted most beautifully. Precisely because her actions were all perfectly unintentional, with absolutely no idea of showing off a beautiful performance, hers was always far more fascinating than stage acting.

Such were my ideas, I must not be misunderstood, and it would be the height of injustice to me to be censured as unfit to be a member of society. A man is sometimes laughed at for acting theatrically. This is all very well, when one derides the folly of undergoing unnecessary self-sacrifices, in order merely to vindicate one's taste; but it is wholly unpardonable for curs, with no idea of what tastes are, to scoff at others by judging things from their own low level. Years ago a youth sought and met Death by leaping over a five hundred foot waterfall. I have an idea that he gave his life that must not be lost, all for the word "aesthetic beauty." Death is heroic in itself; but there is something mysterious in the motives that prompt it. However, it is out of the question for anyone unable to appreciate the heroism of death to laugh at the self-destruction of Fujimura, the youth. Not gifted with the power of grasping the true significance of the heroic ending of life, such a person is bound to fail to resort to the heroic deed, even when circumstances make it most proper, and I conclude, in this sense, that such a one has no right to laugh at Fujimura's tragic death. I am an artist given over wholly to tastes and sentiments, and mingling with others in this mundane world as I may, I am loftier than my vulgar and prosaic neighbours. As a member of society I hold a position from which I may well teach others. I can act more beautifully than those who have no poetry, no painting, no artistic culture. In this man's world a beautiful act is right, just and upright, and he who translates justice, righteousness and uprightness into his doings is a model citizen.

I had walked half a mile upward and came upon a tableland, with trees weaving out the beautiful green of Spring on the North, probably the same which I saw from my room in the Shiota hotel, and which so fascinated me as to bring me out here with my painting kit. I went about this way and that, beating the grass, in search of a place of vantage. I awoke in no time to the fact that the charming scenery I saw from the verandah was, after all, not so easy to take on to a canvas, and besides the colour and atmosphere were changing. The desire to paint slipped away from me, I knew not where. With that ambition gone, it made no difference to me where or how I sat. At random I lay me down on the young grass, the roots of which the Spring sun was bathing with his warm rays, and I thought I was crushing the unseen gossamer.

Presently I lay on my back, with wild dwarf quince blooming all around me. Everything was so transporting that I felt I must write a piece of poetry. I took out my sketch book and wrote down in it, line after line, as they slowly came to me until I had eighteen of them to round it up:

> I left home full of thoughts within me.
> Spring breezes played about my clothes as I
>   came along.
> Sweet is the young grass growing in the
>   wheel tracks.

Neglected paths run into haze are faintly
    visible.
I plant my stick in the ground and look
    around.
Nature is in her robe of clear brightness.
Gentle yellow songsters are hopping to the
    tune of their lovely melody.
Seeing plum blossoms falling like snow.
I walk across the wild field, which is far and
    wide.
Coming upon an old temple, I write a poem
    on its door.
With sorrowful eyes I look up to the cloud,
And see the wild geese homing across the
    sky.
My heart, why so softly quiet?
The past is far back, I forget good or bad.
At thirty I am getting old.
But Spring is lingering.
Strolling about I adapt myself to things
    around.
At other times I drink full of sweet
    fragrance.

I read and reread the lines, pleased that they gave
expression, rather well, to my feelings as I lay among
the vermilion flowers, in sweet oblivion to the cares and
worries of the world. Just then, came "hem," the sound of
somebody clearing the throat, and it took me by
surprise, as I least expected any living soul in my
fairyland. I turned round and saw a man coming out of
the wood screening the brow of the mountain yonder.

He was wearing a felt hat, which shaded his eyes, that I imagined to be looking restlessly about. His indifferent kimono and bare feet almost forced a conclusion that he must be of the fraternity, the members of which are popularly known as tramps. I thought, he might be going down the craggy path I had come up; but no, he retraced his footsteps towards the wood. He did not re-enter the wood, but returned towards the path. In short, he was going backwards and forwards, as if in a walk; but his general appearance told against the latter theory. He was shaking his head now and again, and seemed to be thinking something, now halting, now looking round. Possibly he was expecting somebody, it occurred to me; how should I know?

I could not remove my eyes from the suspicious-looking man, although he aroused no sense of fear or alarm in me. Nor was I seized with any idea of making a picture of him. Nevertheless my eyes were glued to him, in spite of myself. As I was following his every movement, another figure came into the corner of my eye, as the man came to a halt. The two seemed to recognise each other, and my field of vision narrowed as they walked up toward each other, until it became a single point. They stood face to face with a verdant mountain rising on one side, and the out-stretching sea on the other.

One of the pair was, of course, the tramp, and the other a woman. It was Nami-san!

So soon as I recognised Nami-san, I remembered the dagger I saw in her hand that morning. It was possible, even, probable, that she had it with her now, as she stood before the ungainly man. The thought chilled me, unhuman as I was.

The two stood perfectly still, maintaining the same posture as when they first faced each other. They might be talking but I could not hear a word. Presently the man dropped his head forward and Nami-san turned her face toward the mountain. A warbler was singing in that direction, and she seemed to be listening, for all I saw. A few moments later the man straightened himself up, now carrying his head erect, and made a motion as if to walk away. The same moment Nami-san changed her pose and turned her face towards the sea. Something was just visible in the voluminous folds of her obi, it might be the dagger. The man pulled himself up proudly and started to go. Nami-san followed him two or three steps. The man stopped. Did she, perchance, ask him to? In the same moment he turned round, Nami-san thrust her hand into her obi. Mercy! But it was not the dagger it took out, but a purse, the dangling string of which swung gently to and fro in the breeze as the fair hand held it out to the man. One foot planted firmly on the ground and the other a little forward, the upper half of her body slightly thrown backward, and the purple of the purse making a strong contrast with the well shaped hand, the picture was truly worth preserving. But the vision evaporated the moment the man took the purse and disappeared into the wood.

Nami-san gave not a look back to the vanishing man; but she turned right round and walked briskly toward where I lay buried in the flowering quince. "Sensei! Sensei!" She called twice, as soon as she came right in front of me. Wondering when she detected me, I responded:

"What is it, O-Nami-san?"

I held up my head above the quince; my hat had dropped among the grass.

"What can you be doing there, Sensei?"

"I was lying asleep, after a little poetising."

"Now, now, no story-telling, Sensei. You must have seen the show just now?"

"Yes, I took the liberty to see just a little bit of it."

"Ho, ho, ho. Not just a little bit of it, but you should have seen a good deal of it."

"To tell the truth, I saw a good deal of it."

"There you are! Just come out of there, Sensei. Come out of the quince, Sensei."

I meekly obeyed the order.

"Have you got anything more to do in the quince bed?"

"No, nothing more. I was thinking of going home."

"Well, then, we will go home together, Sensei."

I again demonstrated my docility, by going back among the quince, by picking up my hat, by gathering up my kits, and then walking homeward with Nami-san.

"Have you painted anything, Sensei?"

"No, I gave it up."

"You have not painted a single picture since you came to us?"

"No, but don't you see, O-Nami-san, I fled from Tokyo, and having come to a place like this, I must have everything 'go as you like.'"

"Speaking of 'go as you like,' Sensei, life would not be worth living, unless you had it that way, wherever you happen to be. For my part, I am so unconcerned about things that I do not feel ashamed to have a scene like that seen by others."

"No, I do not think you need be ashamed."

"Perhaps, you are right, Sensei; but who do you think that man was?"

"Well, I should imagine he is not a very rich man."

"Ho, ho, ho, you say right, Sensei. You are a good judge. He is in such a pinch that he can no longer remain in Japan, and he came to me for some money."

"Is that so, O-Nami-san? Where did he come from?"

"From the town."

"From so far away? Where is he going, now, O-Nami-san?"

"He told me he was going to Manchuria."

"What for?"

"I don't know, I am sure. He may be going there to make money, or he may be going there to die, for all I know."

I raised my eyes at this point, and looked into my companion's face and there I saw a smile dying away, the meaning of which I did not comprehend.

"He is my husband."

The woman said it with the swiftness of lightning, catching me entirely unguarded. I had not had the faintest idea of trying to get such information out of her. Nor did I expect that she would go the length of telling me all that. She continued:

"Well, Sensei, has it shocked you?"

"Yes, you astonished me somewhat."

"He is not my husband at present. He is my husband from whom I have been divorced."

"Is that so? Well?"

"That is all."

"Well, well. By the by, I saw a fine white house by an orange orchard, which I saw on coming up here. Do you know whose residence that is?"

"It is my brother's. We will stop there on our way home."

"You have some business there?"

"Yes. I must do some errand there."

We came to the craggy path; but instead of going down it, my fair guide led me by turning to the right. After a slow climb of about one hundred yards, we came to a gate. Nami-san waiving the etiquette of knocking at the front door, took me straight into the inner court, which was laid out into a fine garden fronting the main hall of the house. The garden was fenced by a mud walk beyond which extended an orange orchard sloping downward.

"Look, Sensei, isn't this a fine view?"

"Yes, it is fine."

As we sat on the verandah, I espied no sign of anything living in the hall behind us, which was closed from view by paper screens. Nami-san made no attempt to make our presence known to the people of the house, but sat on the verandah, looking down on the orchard with perfect unconcern. This struck me as very strange, and I could not help wondering if she really had any business here. We found no subject to talk about, and sat in silence with our eyes wandering over the orange trees. The sun had almost reached the meridian and the warm sunshine was bathing the whole mountain, while the dark green of the innumerable orange trees below glowed intensely. Presently a loud cock-a-doodle-doo came from the direction of the barn.

"Why, it is noon! I have quite forgotten my errand. Kyuichi-san! Kyuichi-san!"

Nami-san stood up, and, bending forward over the verandah, reached out her hand and slid open a screen. The ten-mat room was empty of any living soul and a pair of hanging pictures by an artist of Kano school lonesomely occupied the tokonoma niche.

"Kyuichi-san!"

A voice coming from somewhere near the barn answered the call, at last, and presently footsteps were heard. They stopped just behind the inner screen. The fusuma opened and at the same moment a plain sheathed dagger went rolling across the matted floor. Nami-san did it so quickly that I did not even see her put her hand in between the folds of her obi and take out the warlike thing. As it was, the dagger stopped just at the foot of Kyuichi-san who had come out of the opening.

"There, that is for you from your uncle as a present for your going to Manchuria."

XIII

We went downstream in a river boat, with Kyuichi-san, to see him off at Yoshida railway station. There were in the boat, beside Kyuichi-san, the old man, Shiota, his erratic daughter, Nami-san, her brother, myself, and also Gembey, who took care of Kyuichi's luggage. I joined the party only to make up the company. I did not quite understand why I should be invited to do so, but being out on an unhuman wandering, there was no need to be scrupulous and so I also went. The boat had a flat bottom, as if built on a raft. The old man sat in the centre, Nami-san and I in front of him, Kyuichi and Nami-san's brother behind him, and Gembey by himself with the luggage in the stern.

"Are you fond of War?" asked Nami-san.

"I shan't be able to tell until I am in it. There may be times I may find it very hard; but at others I may be jolly about it," answered Kyuichi, who had never before been to war.

"However hard, you must know that it is for the state and your country," commented the old man.

"With such a warlike thing as a dagger given you, don't you wish to begin fighting?" asked Nami-san in her cynical way.

"That may be, but...."

The light response made the old man laugh shaking his beard, while his son looked as if he heard nothing.

"Do you mean to say that you can go and fight in battle with such an indifferent mind?" pressed Nami-san, holding her pretty face before Kyuichi, whose eyes met those of Nami-san's brother at the same instant.

"I am sure Nami-san would make a grand warrior, if she became one," came from the woman's brother, as the very first word spoken to her in the boat. Judging from the tone in which it was said, one might have suspected that it was not meant to be merely a joke.

"I? I become a soldier? If I could, I would have become one long ago. I would have been dead by this time. Kyuichi-san you had better make up your mind to be killed. You would gain nothing by coming home alive."

"Come, now, no more of your raving.... You must come home in triumph, nephew, dying is not the only way to serve the country. I am good for three or four years more yet. We will again meet in joy."

The old gentleman's word tapered and softened till they melted into unseen tears, which he concealed from us. Kyuichi said nothing; but turned his eyes toward the left bank of the river, where they met those of a man with a rod and line before him. It was fortunate that the angler did not ask Kyuichi why he looked so sad.

Our boat glided down with delightful smoothness, the willow trees on the embankments on either side, flitting backward as rustic airs came wafting, probably from the young damsels at the weaving machines in houses little yonder, gently stirring the silence of the calm Spring afternoon.

"Sensei, won't you paint my picture?" demanded Nami-san, as her brother and Kyuichi were engrossed in soldiery topics, while the old gentleman had started journeying to dreamland.

"Why, with pleasure," I answered, taking out my sketch book and writing down in it:

> *"Harukazeni sora toke shusuno meiwa*
> *nani?"*[44]

Nami-san curtsied, smiling, and said: "Not a single stroke sketch like this, but a carefully executed production, giving expression to my spirit and character, Sensei."

"I wish I could oblige you with all my heart; but to be frank, your face, as it is, would not make a picture."

"Thanks for your compliments. But what am I to do to make myself fit for a picture?"

"Don't get angry, O-Nami-san; I can make a fine picture of you at this very moment. But there is something wanting in your expression, and it will be a great pity to portray you without that something."

"Something wanting? That cannot be helped, as I cannot be anything else but what I am born with."

"You may be born with; but the face may look in all sorts of ways."

"At your own pleasure?"

"Yes."

"The idea! Don't you make a fool of me, because you think I am only a woman."

"Why, now I say all this, because you are a woman."

"Eh? Show me, then, Sensei, how you can make your face look in all sorts of ways."

"You have seen enough of me of being made to look in all sorts of ways day after day."

Nami-san said no more, but turned the other way. The embankments had disappeared, the riversides being now almost level with the surface of the stream. The rice growing lowlands on either side, which had not yet been ploughed, had turned into a sea of rouge, with the wild red milk-vetch in full bloom. The pink sea stretched limitlessly till it was swallowed up in the distant haze. The eyes that followed up the haze, saw a high peak, halfway up which, a soft, dreamy cloud of Spring was issuing.

"That is the mountain the rear of which you scaled in coming up to Nakoi, Sensei," said Nami-san, as her fair hand pointed toward the mountain that towered into the sky like a vision of Spring.

"Is the 'Hobgoblin Cliff' about there?"

"You see that purple spot under that deep green?"

"That shaded place, you mean?"

"Is it a shaded place? It must be a bared patch."

"No, it must be a hollow; a bared patch would look more brown."

"That may be. Anyhow, the rock is said to be about there."

"Then the 'Seven Bends' must be a little to the left."

"No, the Seven Bends is a good bit further away, it being in another mountain, which is beyond that one."

"That is so; but it must be in the direction, where a light sheet of cloud is hanging."

"Yes, in that direction, Sensei."

The old man's arm resting on the side of the boat slipped, and that awoke him. He asked if the destination had not been reached, and he gave himself up to yawning, which act took the shape of putting out the chest, bending the doubled right elbow backward, and stretching the left arm full length forward, in short going through a form of archery. Nami-san burst out laughing.

"This is my way...."

"You must be fond of archery," I said laughing.

The aged spa-hotel man volunteered to tell me that he made only a toy of ordinary bows in his days, and his arms were pretty sure even in his old age, patting his left shoulder as he said this. Talk of war was at its height behind him.

Our boat was now fast reaching its destination, the vetch adorned field having given way to rows of houses, then to lumber yards, shops, eating houses and so on. Swallows flitted over the stream, and ducks quacked in the water. In no time we got out of our boat and headed for the railway station.

I was at last dragged back into the living world. I call it the living world, where railway trains may be seen. I am of opinion that there is nothing else that represents the twentieth century civilization so truly as the railway train. It packs hundreds of people in a box, and they have no choice but to be transported all at the same uniform speed, in complete disregard of individuality. The twentieth century strives to develop individuality to its utmost, and then goes about crushing this individuality in every conceivable way, saying you are free in this lot of so many by so many feet, but that you must not set a foot outside the encircling fence, as in the case of railway train prisoners. But the iron fence is unbearably galling to all with any sense of individuality, and they are all roaring for liberty, day and night. Civilization gives men liberty and makes them strong as a tiger. It then entraps and keeps them encaged. It calls this peace. But this is not a real peace. It is a peace like that of the tiger in the menagerie, which is lying quietly as he looks calmly over the crowd that gathers round his cage. Let a single bar of the cage be out of its place and darkness will descend on the earth. A second French Revolution will then break out. Individual revolutions are even now breaking out. Ibsen has given us instances of the way in which this revolution will burst forth. However, this opinion of railway train can hardly embellish my sketch book, and still less may I impart it openly to others. So I kept my peace and joined my companions in stopping at a refreshment room in front of the railway station.

There were two countrymen in their straw sandals, sitting on stools near us, one of them wrapped in a red blanket, and the other wearing a pair of old fashioned native trousers of diverse colours, with one of his hands over the largest patch, which made the combination of variegation of black, red, yellow particularly conspicuous.

One of them was saying: "No good, after all, eh?"

"No, not a bit good."

"Pity that man is not given two stomachs like the bovine."

"All would be well if we had two. Why, all you have to do, then, will be to cut out one of them if it goes wrong."

I thought the countrymen, at least one of them, must be a victim of stomach trouble. They know not even the smell of winds howling over the Manchurian battlefield. They see nothing wrong in modern civilization. They probably know not what revolution means, having never heard even the word itself. They are perhaps, not quite sure that they have got one or two stomachs in them. I took out my book and sketched them.

Clang, clang went the bell at the station. The ticket had already been bought for Kyuichi with the platform tickets.

"Now let us go," says Nami-san standing up.

"All right," joined the old gentleman, suiting his action to his words, and we trooped out of the refreshment room, into the station, then past the wicket to the platform. The bell was ringing.

The monster snake of civilization came rumbling into the station, gliding over the shining rails. The snake was puffing black smoke from its mouth.

"Now be good," said old Mr. Shiota.

"Goodbye," returned Kyuichi-san bowing his head.

"Go and meet your death," says cynical Nami-san again.

The snake stopped in front of us and many doors on its side opened. Many people came out and many went in, Kyuichi being one of the latter. The old gentleman, Nami-san's brother, Nami-san, and I, all stood near the edge of the platform.

Once the wheels turned, Kyuichi-san would no more be one of "our" world, but would be going to far, far away country, where men are struggling among the fumes of smoke and powder, and slipping and rolling unreasonly in something red and the sky is screeching with detonations. Kyuichi-san, who was going to a world of that weird sort, stood motionless in his car, gazing at us in silence. The bond of relations between us and Kyuichi-san, who caused us to come out here was to break here, was, in fact, breaking momentarily. The door of the car still stood open as did the car window, and we were looking at each other, with only six feet between the going and the stopping; but that was all that remained of the bond, which was every second snapping.

The conductor came along quickly closing the doors, each door shut increasing the distance between the going and the stopping. Bang closed Kyuichi-san's car door, and we now stood in two different worlds. The old gentleman unconsciously brought himself close up to the car window and the young man held out his head.

"Look out there!" The train began to move almost before the words were finished, the sound of the engine working, coming in measured rhythm at first, gradually gaining in speed. One by one the car windows passed us and Kyuichi-san's face grew smaller and smaller. The last third class car rolled before us, and just at that moment another head appeared out of its window.

The unshaven face of the "tramp" peered out from under a worn-out brown soft hat, casting a sad lingering look. The eyes of Nami-san and of the deserted one met unintentionally. The train was moving out in earnest.

The face at the window disappeared instantly. Nami-san stood abstractedly, gazing after the departing train. Strangely enough, in that abstracted look of hers, I saw that missing "compassion and pity" visibly outstanding, that I had never seen before.

"That is the stuff! You've got it. With that coming, it will make a picture."

I said this in a low voice as I patted Nami-san on her back. That moment I completed the plan of my picture.

ENDNOTES

1. Noh is a peculiarly Japanese stage performance of ancient origin, from which sprang the latter-day theatrical plays. It is presented on its own stage to the enjoyment of those who love to see human actions reduced to dreamy gracefulness, beautiful curves, and melodious sweetness. ↩

2. Basho Matsuo was the founder of his own school of Hokku and one of the most famous poets Japan has produced. He was a seer in his way. Born in 1644, he died in 1694. ↩

3. Hokku, also called Haiku, is an ode consisting of only seventeen Japanese kana syllables, and makes a point of compressing into a couple of lines an impression made by the outside world, thoughts aroused by an event, sentiments felt and all else that affects human heart. In fact, everything that carries poetical sentiments and is uttered in poetical tune within seventeen syllables makes a hokku. It may be a mere whim, an instantaneous

impression, or else a very deep thought; but a good hokku is always rich in colour and profound in idea, which it leaves unsaid but only hints, and at least arouses a train of fancies in the reader. ↵

4. *Danna-sama* is a term originally adopted from Sanskrit *Dana*, meaning "exhibition of charity" and is used in addressing a man of position. Stands for English Sir, Master, or Your Honour; but nearer French Monsieur. Less formally it takes the form of *Danna-san* or simply *Danna*. ↵

5. A small yellowish-green warbler, that sings with a peculiarly sweet note, generally but wrongly identified with the English nightingale. The *uguisu* never sings at night, as does the English bird, except as a caged captive under a paper cover, with a light burning near. ↵

6. Means an old woman or a grandmother with an honorific *O*; *Bah-san* is less formal. ↵

7. Inen was a disciple of Basho and a passionate lover of nature in her quietude. ↵

8.   "Hark, the packhorse bells in the
            Spring breeze,
            Even as they jingled in Inen's ear."

    ↵

9. A rustic air sung by a *mago* or packhorse driver and the like, always arousing pastoral associations of peace and care-freeness. ↵

10.   "List, *mago-uta*, grey hair undyed
                  Spring is going again."

↵

11. *Oba* means aunt and *san* a honorific affix less formal than *sama*. *Oba-san* is used in its broadest sense as is aunt. ↵

12. Aki is the name of a woman; in this case that of the old woman's married daughter. *O* and *san* are respectively an honorific prefix and affix. ↵

13. *Jo* is daughter with the honorific *sama*, which becomes *san* less formally. ↵

14.   "Wise that the bride went
                  After the flower season on horse
                      back."

   This haiku was probably suggested by an old ditty: "Why tie a horse to a blossoming cherry tree? The flowers will scatter if spirited the horse becomes."
↵

15. Same as *O-Bah-san*, only less polite. See <u>6</u>. ↵

16.   "Even like the dew drop
              That when autumn comes,
           Lodges trembling on grass
              So must I roll off to die."

↩

17. Obi is a lined belt, made of fabric of various texture used over the kimono, going two or three times round the waist. The Japanese woman's obi is often made of very beautiful material, and is about eight-tenths of a foot in width and thirteen feet or so in length, so that it is a ponderous affair to wear round the waist. ↩

18. The semitransparent paper screen, sliding in grooves and serving the purposes of light-admitting doors in Japanese houses. ↩

19. "The crazy thing, it shakes dew drops off the aronia?" A blossoming aronia wet in rain is often sung as a beauty in ablution. Crazy must therefore be anyone who shakes dew drop off an aronia in bloom. ↩

20. "Shadow of a flower; shadow of a woman; both so misty!" An instantaneous picture of woman standing by a blossoming tree in the dim moonlight. ↩

21. "The Reynard in woman's guise, the moon so misty." The fox is often spoken of as "Shoichi-i,"

which is the title of the Inari god, who is always associated with the animal. The fancy here is that the moon being so soft and dim that it will give the cunning animal an opportunity to assume a human figure, and the woman may be a fox in disguise. ↵

22. "A garland she makes of the midnight stars of Spring." ↵

23. "It is Beauty loosening and bathing her hair in the clouds of a Spring night." ↵

24. "Spring's night this, how fair the singing one." ↵

25. "Spirit of aronia lured out even the moonlit night." ↵

26. "Song rises and falls, with Spring sauntering under the moon." ↵

27. "How so alone, when fullest Spring is ripening!" ↵

28. Same as shoji, only mounted with wallpaper like stuff and therefore heavier. It also moves in grooves and takes the place of a door in Japanese houses. ↵

29. A shoji is often put in windows in Japanese houses. ↵

30. In Japan it is considered nothing extraordinary or improper for hotel maids or others of the sex,

waiting on a guest, to help him to put on a kimono. ↵

31. Zen is the name of a Buddhist sect, credited with rising above worldly trammels. ↵

32. "Dews on aronia fly; 'tis morning raven." ↵

33. "Shadowy the shadow of flower and the shadow of woman." ↵

34. "Shadow of flower doubled the shadow of woman." ↵

35. "It is lordling in woman's guise in misty moonlight." ↵

36. The three stringed Japanese guitar, often called *Sangen* nowadays. ↵

37. Generally means a Buddhist priest, implying respect. *Osho-san* is a less formal form. ↵

38. Same as *karakami.* ↵

39. A term of widest application. Scholars, teachers, savants men of profession or of speciality are all Sensei. ↵

40. Same as *Danna-sama*, only less polite. See 4. ↵

41. A round-head Buddhist priest, often pronounced "bonze" by Westerners. ↵

42. Buddhist priests from the youngest to the oldest keep their head clean shaved all over. ↵

43. Same as *karakami*. See 28. ↵

44.   "Even as the gate of heaven opens
              In the Spring breeze, fair one!
           Show what is in your heart."

    ↵